ISBN 978-1-331-75965-2
PIBN 10231031

This book is a reproduction of an important historical work. Forgotten Books uses
state-of-the-art technology to digitally reconstruct the work, preserving the original format
whilst repairing imperfections present in the aged copy. In rare cases, an imperfection in
the original, such as a blemish or missing page, may be replicated in our edition. We do,
however, repair the vast majority of imperfections successfully; any imperfections that
remain are intentionally left to preserve the state of such historical works.

1 MONTH OF
FREE
READING

at

www.ForgottenBooks.com

By purchasing this book you are eligible for one month membership to ForgottenBooks.com, giving you unlimited access to our entire collection of over 700,000 titles via our web site and mobile apps.

To claim your free month visit:
www.forgottenbooks.com/free231031

From the Author

David Guthrie Esq
Robert's friend & mine
1st December
1865

ITOYENNE JACQUELINE

IN THREE VOLUMES

" Old footsteps trod the upper floors,
  Old faces looked in through the doors,
  Old voices called me from without."

  TENNYSON.

CITOYENNE JACQUELINE

A Woman's Lot in the Great French Revolution

By SARAH TYTLER

VOLUME I.

Anchora Spei

ALEXANDER STRAHAN, PUBLISHER

148, STRAND, LONDON

1865

Robert

WITH LOVE THAT CANNOT DIE
HERE AND YONDER

CONTENTS.

———◆———

CITOYENNE JACQUELINE

VOLUME I.

CITOYENNE JACQUELINE.

CHAPTER I.

THE TOUR DE FAYE — A CARD PARTY AND A RESTLESS CITOYENNE.

THE early summer of 1792 was ripening the wheat-ears and darkening the vine leaves about the hamlet of Faye-aux-Jonquilles. The season was too far advanced, however, for showing the appropriateness of its sweet-smelling name, or for proving that it had contributed in its day to the four thousand crowns' worth of jonquilles spent on the progress of the Great Monarch to Chantilly, which is pleasantly chronicled by that jonquille among French women — Madame de Sevigné.

But Faye was lucky in more than its name of Faye-among-the-Jonquilles. It had plump wheat-ears instead of the shrivelled heads of rye which re-placed, at a later date, the jonquilles that enamelled and perfumed the steps of the sublime Louis. Its present proprietors had suffered less than some from the road-making, the charge on salt, and the general taxes of the French people, which took somewhat from the scent of the jonquilles and the sublimity of the Louis.

Faye was in the interior of France, sixty miles from Paris. It was nothing to speak of in size. A score of thatched cottages, some of them of dry mud, but none of them more than moderately miserable ; an old inn ; and a little church, not yet closed, with square tower and red roof. The three con-stituents of a hamlet were fairly represented in it — the green-stained fountain in the centre, where men and women lounged and gossipped, and washed their onions and radishes, and shred their cabbages, in the evenings ; the posting-house — to wit, the bulged-out old inn ; the prison, traditionally held to be the dungeons of the little castle on the rising ground at the end of the village. A rough road, bordered by walnut trees, wound and clomb to the Tour de Faye, giving one the impression that the village rose on tip-toe to curtsey to the feudal lord and master, in spite of the prohibition of titles of rank by a National Assembly, and the flight of great flocks of nobles.

The Tour was a true antique, not setting its claim on massiveness or splendour. It had the hoary picturesque grace of a grey lichen, set between the green of the earth and the blue, or daffodil, or pea-bloom of the sky. The walls were very thick, and pierced with narrow windows. They looked as if they might have stood sieges from the Normans and the English, the League and the Fronde ; and as if they might yet stand another siege from a new Jacquerie. There were two tourelles, connected by the nucleus of a main tower, crowned by an unequal, high-peaked roof, with a handful of girouettes, or weathercocks,

thrown into the bargain. A morsel of bocage—
what remained of the chase and the fields of
the Faye domain—stretched out in the background. On one side a terrace, with a flight
of shallow steps, led down into the garden, the
stateliness and precision of whose clipped cypresses
and yews contrasted broadly with the wild luxu-
riance of its thickets of lovely red and white
roses. The two tourelles were, so far as regarded
their internal economy, perfectly self-contained,
and had been named, centuries before the Revolution, the tourelle of Monsieur, and the tourelle
of Madame. Monsieur's tourelle held the char-
ter room, Monsieur's cabinet, and Monsieur's
bedroom. Madame's tourelle held a morning
room, Madame's boudoir, and Mademoiselle's bedroom. The salle and the guest-chambers were in
the connecting link of the main tower, over the
arched doorway. There was a sunk flat, with a
vaulted kitchen and red-rusted cellars, reputed to
have been dungeons. The servants' closets were
niched in anywhere and everywhere, and were
not counted in the plan. No doubt, the arrange-

ments were all according to native ideas of order and propriety, though certainly they "knew not the comfortable."

Citizen Faye had not swum with the great tide of aristocratic emigration. He had family reasons. He was a philosopher himself, to begin with,—that was when he did not exactly expect the sans-culottes to proceed from theory to practice. He was living on sufferance, shorn of his plumes, and pinched in his diet, with the prospect of becoming still more a beggar, and of dining at the table without the tablecloth, should he ever venture to Paris.

The simple inhabitants of Faye had not yet imagined anything so fashionable and distinguished as a scaffold in its own person rising up, and becoming the leading spectacle, in their tame provincial experience. They were far back, these peasant proprietors. They were not even big enough for a National Guard of their own. They had to go to the next town to see the Altar of Liberty, and to swear to the Social Contract. Their single glory was, that Jonquille, the son of the innkeeper

La Sarte, was the deputy for their department of
Mousse.   But in the face of this fact, so great was
the force of habit, that when Monsieur de Faye, in
his redingote and ruffles, strolled down in the
midst of the children, of the goats and the hens,
and stood still to speak to this or that goodman,
then Citizen Joiner or Citizen Blacksmith would
pluck the cap from his head, even to the tune
of the far-away yet swelling cry, " Liberty,
Equality, Fraternity!" shouted by the orators up
in Paris.

Monsieur (still Monsieur within the Tour walls)
went every evening between five and six to kiss
Madame's hand, ask her how she did, and play
cards with her and his daughter—their only
child — till supper was served at eight.   The
family were thus playing cards one evening in
June, 1792.

Madame's room was warm, and heavily perfumed.
There was a glowing wood fire on the hearth-dogs,
and the open window in the embrasure only tem-
pered the heat.   Before the window, on a stand,
were pots with late violets and lilies of the valley,

and, in small tubs, two forced orange trees in full blossom. Above the orange trees were cages of canaries, both full fledged and newly hatched, which kept up a continual warbling and twittering.   There were strips of Persian carpet on the clear polished floor; mirrors in filagree frames; a harpsichord; family portraits of women with powdered hair, and men in lace cravats and half armour.   There were soft, deep easy chairs, and a low, broad sofa, besides chairs of gilt ebony, with cushions in tambour work.   There was provision for Madame's devotion in a draped recess, furnished with an ivory crucifix, and thin books of hours, bearing forbidden shields on their covers; and for her handiwork, in a mouton or heap of gold lace, the threads of which she unpicked with all the grace, skill, and dignified industry of a parfileuse, or unpicker of gold thread, which had been the only employment for grand dames in Madame's youth, and which they put to profit by selling its bullion fruit in the regular market.   There was a rich, though tarnished, trailing ruby velvet curtain veiling the door.   But the great feature in the room was an immense four-post bed, seven feet every way, with gauze and silk curtains, and a white satin quilt, embroidered with huge stately convolvuluses and carnations.   Madame was still partial to receptions in that bed, on which occasions she wore a white jacket and white gloves, and had the card table so placed that she could join in the game without difficulty or awkwardness.

Altogether, if ever there was a noble, sensuous, quaint setting to a party of card-players, it was the boudoir of Madame.   And it may please those who love to be tickled with the keen flavour of danger in the wind, to reflect, as they look on all such family groups lingering in France in the year of grace 1792, that the sword of Damocles hung over them, suspended by the single hair.   Not only over Monsieur and his superannuated major-domo, who were the men of the party, but over Madame, over Mademoiselle — ay, over the very old waiting woman, Agathe, and the young waiting woman, Babette, if they dared to shelter master or mistress.

Monsieur was stout and grizzled—those foes

to romantic illusion, — yet nobody could have mistaken him, nobody could have forgotten him. There was a grand air, not only in his Bourbon long nose and double chin, in the carriage of his head and the wave of his hand, but in the very curl of his lip and the droop of the heavy eyelids over his hollow eyes. He was never in dishabille either of mind or body; he must have put on and off his damask suit as Louis did his wig— curled and powdered to the last puff—in bed and with the curtains drawn. He never fretted or fumed at Madame; to her he was always courtly, bland, and agreeable. Possibly he had his errors and deficiencies, like the amiable and delightful Frenchman of whom most people have heard, who would have been perfect except for the flaw of occasionally poisoning a friend. But the sentence was true, applied to Monsieur, that "men never grew old till the Revolution. Before then they had no wearisome infirmities. When they had gout, they walked as though they had it not, and without making faces; they hid suffering by a good education."

Madame had possessed birth and beauty, and, what is more valued than either in France, **wit**, when all these had more than their full prestige. Both in body and mind she was now made up **too** elaborately, yet not unsuccessfully. The brilliant rouge, and the perruque with the hair piled high above the forehead, and the plume of feathers above the hair, agreed with the silver and blue brocade and the hoop—the fashion of Madame's prosperity, and the fashion of her adversity. She sat with her fan on one arm, and a diamond snuff-box within easy reach of her disengaged hand. She was full of airs, but they were delightfully subtle, and dashed with natural humour; and she was frank and candid in the midst of her affectation. She told stories of the Porcheron balls, where she had gone for a frolic, and danced with her lacquey; and of Madame Dudevant's bureau, when Madame's biting wit was only second **to** that of Voltaire. If Monsieur was not present, she would describe how she had met him first the evening before their nuptials, and how she, a girl of fifteen fresh from her convent, had been frightened by his plume, his sword-knot (Monsieur was a mousquetaire), and his curious glances; not understanding then that there was nothing to fear. Monsieur and she, born and brought up as they had been, could not do other than behave becomingly to each other, Madame would say, with a loftiness that was at the same time inexpressibly easy.

Those figures were of old France. Mademoiselle, on her stool opposite them, was of young France. The French have it that a woman cannot be two things at once, and so not a prude at twenty. But Jacqueline de Faye was a great many things at sixteen; she was a philosopher, a fine lady, half a nun, and a whole passionate, sentimental girl. However, her education had been exceptional, and charged with transition, like the times. She had been reared at home instead of in the traditional convent; she had been played with by her father in fanciful philanthropic. and metaphysical discussions; she had been talked to by her mother; she had been confirmed by the curé; she had read on

her own account "Paul and Virginia" and
" Melanie," and longed to live according to
nature in the Mauritius; to have tamarinds and
pines for cherries and walnuts, the Fan Palm
River for the Faye stream, and the Shaddock
Grove Church for the village church near the
willows. She could have even found it in her
heart to wish that her little lion dog were
transformed into Fidêle, and Agathe and Paul
into such faithful negroes as Dominique and
Mary. And oh! above all, should she ever find
a slim, dark, dutiful, devoted Paul? Was there
anybody in the world like Paul? Was there
a chevalier, and was his name Achille? If
she could only go to the Mauritius and try life
according to nature there! But she was an
honest little girl, and she was afraid that even
though Monsieur, and Madame, and Babette,
and above all Achille, accompanied her, she would
miss the Paris *Mercury*, and the fresh news, and
ribands.

The Revolution was making strange work with
women, when Manon Phlippon, among the etch-

ing tools and copper-plates of the engraver's dark little shop in Paris, and Charlotte Corday, beneath the elms in the cloisters of the abbey at Caen, were renouncing their Prayer-books for Plutarch's Lives. When Germaine Neckar, with her harsh, bizarre features and great black eyes, like blazing torches, was improvising and addressing on politics and literature the startled *blasé* men and women in the wealthy banker's saloons of the tottering capital. When Théroigne Mérincourt, the courtesan, in the red riding-habit and hat and feather, was decreed a sabre for having led the mob at the taking of the Bastille, and for being the first on the bastion.

And Jacqueline was of young France down to her looks and costume. Her beauty was not her mother's beauty; her distinction was not her father's stateliness. Her forehead was more full than broad. Her nose was straight and somewhat short, but so also was her upper lip. Her mouth pouted, and smiled as only pouting mouths can smile. Her bright colour was all in her mouth although her round face was very fresh, soft, and healthful. There was a dreamy expression on her forehead, and a sweet, vague wistfulness in her mouth when it remained at rest, notwithstanding her eyes being the clear hazel eyes,—part hazel, part grey,—which seem to strike fire with disdain or anger. And, by the way, the French do very well to admire this lovely moorland colour in eyes, but they do very ill to call it green. She wore her own hair, thrown back and falling in long light-brown curls on her shoulders, according to the last mode. She had no hoop. Her gown—a heavy brocade like Madame's, but coffee-coloured in place of sky-blue, girls never appearing in full dress save in the attire of novices,—had still a train, which was drawn through both pocket-holes, showing her worked petticoat and pretty feet, on which the buckles twinkled. A fine white muslin neckerchief was crossed over her bosom, and there was a breast-knot just under her dainty chin. She was as exquisitely picturesque as a shepherdess of Durfé's, done to Madame Pompadour's orders in a tableau on a piece of Sévres china. But there was a busy brain throbbing and straining itself under the rippled hair over head; a warm, pitiful heart, heaving and swelling to meet the brave breastknot.

Behind the three principal figures were the major-domo, Paul—rheumatic, vinegar-faced, and spindle-legged, a martinet in a short-waisted and short-tailed coat, and knee-breeches of grey cloth, to be as little like livery as possible, but retaining the short sword at his side; and Agathe, Madame's woman—red-haired, morose, in a stuff gown and little cap, so formal and sombre that she might have belonged to an order of nuns when nuns were in favour; and Babette. The first two were mere cool shadows, relieving the brilliant figures in the foreground. But Babette, who vindicated the rights of the people, and was only three years older than her young mistress, was more than a shadow.

Babette was strong and thickset. She was brown as a berry; had a wide mouth, a flat nose, a forehead not above a quarter of an

inch in height ; and she was continually diminish-
ing that quarter of an inch by drawing it up into
three clear-cut wrinkles when she made a face of
astonishment or protest. These wrinkles would
be ploughed furrows in her brow before she
was thirty. But she had the longest curving eye-
lashes, shading eyes as black as sloes, and rest·
ing on ripe cheeks; the whitest teeth ; the most
symmetrical pillar of a throat. In her golden
brown petticoat, her crimson apron with a bib,
her lace cap without ribands, but with lappets
hanging down on each shoulder, yet not conceal-
ing her gold earrings, she was delightful to
look upon ; and it was refreshing to be ac-
quainted with her. She was intensely practical in
her views, but at the same time she had imagina-
tion, she had raillery, she had lively affections.
Standing behind little Mademoiselle, and combing
vigorously the white silken mane of Mademoiselle's
little lion dog Nerina—too wise to resist the
rousing process in her hands,—she was herself,
and could not be anybody else, or be
melted into the being of another, without the

Tour de Faye losing a ray of broad, strong, open-air sunshine.

The players lost and won, and continued the struggle, as players are wont to do in the game of life. Monsieur and Madame were pleasantly interested. Jacqueline, the representative of young France, was a little rude, naturally; cared less for loto than she should have cared; but was restrained from expressing her feelings by the great deference which French children paid to their parents. She no more dreamt of yawning than an English child of flinging the cards in her father's or mother's face. In an interval between the deals, Paul handed round frothed chocolate and mareschino on a silver tray with armorial bearings—three falcons and two savages —not yet confiscated, or buried in the garden. Mademoiselle profited by the diversion, but soon the interminable round of abstracts, ambros, terns, and quaterns, recommenced.

Then a nightingale out in the bocage began suddenly to trill its plaintive ditty. The sound was very foreign to the scene. And just because of

that, Mademoiselle's young heart responded by
listening spellbound, by wondering, growing pensive, wayward, and wild.   Her occupation became
more and more distasteful to her, her attention
strayed, the heat of the room flushed her fair
cheek, the perfume caused her youthful head to
ache.   Like Sterne's starling, she could have
cried, "I can't get out, I can't get out;" but she
was dutiful, noble, and, *noblesse oblige*, she made
no sign.

"I remember playing thus at cards once, when
Saxe came in a crac from one of his campaigns,"
observed Madame.   "He was barbarous that man,
though he was a hero.   He wanted us to give
over playing, that he might write a despatch ; but
the Abbé Dubois told him, 'Monsieur the Marshal, the French are not used to stir on account of
the enemy.   There is enough of room in the world
both for our game and your campaign.'   And the
Abbé had the best of it, though Saxe swore great
raw oaths, as he ate raw cabbage, like a German.
The Abbé never failed at the repartee.   When the
Jacobins seized him the other day, and shouted

'To the lamp-post!' he answered, 'Very well, my friends; but will you see the better for me?' Even the Republicans had the taste to let him off for the speech; but unfortunately he was assassinated in the next square before he had time to speak. His hour had struck; it did not signify," Madame ended, composedly.

A moment afterwards, Madame showed herself ruffled, and gave an elegant wave of her cards towards the cages with the birds, from which a little croaking cry made itself heard. "Agathe, I wish you would look to Eglantine. There is something vexing him. I am sure of it. For these two days, he has not been himself. He makes his breast like a drum. Either his seed is too old, or his pebble of sugar is too hard. He gives me trouble. And then there is Rosette. She will neglect her little ones. Ah! I have nothing left to care for now but my birds, because I made up my mind, when Nerina's mother died, that I ought not to have her place refilled. I could live and die easier without another darling of a dog."

"I hope your birds repay you the trouble they cost," remarked Monsieur, without the least tone of offence. On the contrary, he proceeded to inquire, with polite interest, "Do they thrive, Madame?"

"Well, it seems when one has only a single thing, that thing must do its best to plague its proprietor. My child, if you make faces in that way I shall faint; I cannot stand mows."

The last apostrophe was addressed to Jacqueline, who was involuntarily biting her lips.

"My little one," said her father, "a demoiselle's life is too short, and her face too important, to admit of mows."

"Sacristie, Monsieur!" broke in Babette, without ceremony. "Don't you see, Mademoiselle has the cramps? Young joints are not like old ones, nor young blood neither. Mademoiselle is like Eglantine, she is pining for a breath of fresh air, and a turn of a walk, since there are no plays and balls for her. It is she who will faint, if you confine her longer here."

The freedom of speech allowed to servants in

French households, from Moliére's time down-
wards, was a safety-valve which, under the old
régime, prevented the domestic life of the country
from losing altogether the trifle called human
nature.

"Thanks," Madame even acknowledged graciously. "But no, Babette, assuredly my daughter
is not so vulgar."

To faint at mows, and to be faint for fresh air,
were two very different things.

"For me," added Madame, "I never cared for
that dish, nature. Taken by itself, it is as a salad
without roast before it, or Neufchâtel cheese after
it."

"Pardon, Madame," interposed Monsieur, ele-
vating his eyebrows; "I thought the ladies liked
everything for a change."

"That depends on whether the change is worth
the pains," explained Madame, candidly. "Let
us go on, Jacqueline."

But Monsieur and Madame were good-natured
and indulgent when there was no question of
interest or honour. At the close of the next

game there fell from both of them, alternately, "Say, then, is it so, my child?" "Then go away: for us, we will play picquet till supper." "But how barbarous you are! What tastes! To go out when the sun is going to bed, except to pay visits before the comedy, and in the country! Fy! there will be the milking of cows, and the dew, and the snails. I always hated sensibility. I always said it would ruin France."

Jacqueline accepted the accusation of being barbarous without demur, and made her curtsey. Madame uttered a little scream, and called her back to make it over and over again, till Jacqueline's knees ached with weariness, while her ears tingled with a running fire of criticism from Madame, and mockery from Monsieur: how like a shot partridge the child was; how she was even as Madame Neckar, who was bad on the legs, could not sit down, and slept standing; how she should walk through a minuet with a sheep for a partner, to cure her of looking as if she were going to bleat; what the old Duke de Rochefoucault had once said of poor Madame

de Longueville's dancing—that it was for the air,
not the gross earth : — till Jacqueline's cheeks,
albeit used to such a fire, were red as her lips, when
Madame wound up by informing her she needed
rouge to prevent the world seeing that she blushed
like a peasant. And Monsieur called out finally,
" Good evening, Mademoiselle. My bear, do not
hug me. No, my doll, do not lose your balance,
or your nose may be shattered; though it is not
much in the way;—who knows? If not, we will
read the *Henriade* together, to-morrow, you and
I. Parbleu! there are some paragraphs about
the season of St. Bartélémi's day I have reason
to get by heart."

Jacqueline got out of the door; executed something like an entrechat in the vestibule, little
philosopher though she was ; skipped down the
tourelle stair, leaving Babette to bring her the
curled bunch of feathers which served her for a
hat, and, together with the long gloves, constituted her walking dress. At last she set out,
attended by Babette, to learn what tune the
nightingale was singing to her, and what mes-

sage the evening star was bringing for her. Loto and Court gossip were all very well at a time; but, like Paris mud, their smell was sharp to young nostrils, and there was something more in heaven and earth for a girl of sixteen to dream of.

CHAPTER II.

JACQUELINE took a turn along the terrace with her hands folded before her, her eyes raised to the sky. Babette walked by her side. The nightingale's song caused her to yearn after she knew not what; to feel as if she could die of the harmony which stirred the dumb, slumbering depths of her soul.

Babette counted the strokes of the Tour clock as it struck six, glanced down at a roll in her lap, and speculated when Mademoiselle would tire of the promenade, and leave her to follow her own devices.

But there was more to be heard than the nightingale: the landrails from the fields beyond the bocage, and the frogs from the fishponds, rattled and croaked a homely domestic duet, breaking in . on the mysterious solo which spoke of love and death and everlasting constancy. Jacqueline liked the duet too, though it woke her from a vision, for she was kindly as well as tender ; and in place of growing ecstatic or maudlin, her mood changed like lightning. She turned briskly to the other girl, in order to prattle and play with her.

"What have you there, Babette? Why did you wish to get away by yourself, my rabbit? Where are you going, and will you take me with you?"

Babette stood still and looked at Mademoiselle. She saw there was no use trying to deceive her mistress when she turned up her little nose in that fashion, and when her eyes sparkled, shone, and pierced every obstacle opposed to them. And Babette, besides, was quite of opinion that there was no use trying to deceive when nobody would believe her. She therefore set herself to answer the easiest question.

"Is it this bagatèlle in my lap you mean, Mademoiselle? It is a small piece of fine linen that I span. My faith! how my arms ached!" And she rubbed her rough, dimpled elbows. "The citizen Robinet wove it into a charming little web. What trouble I had to hide it from Agathe! She would have sworn that I, an honest girl, of honest people, took it out of the linen press; she who says as many prayers as La Sarte, and prowls and picks for ever in Madame's wardrobe. She has not her red hair for nothing. 'Distrust the red' is a safe proverb."

Jacqueline was not to be wiled from the gratification of her lawful curiosity.

"But what have you to do with little webs of linen, Babette? Is it possible that you are going to be married without telling me?"

"Hein! no!" denied Babette, reducing her low forehead to two-and-a-half tight cords, and accompanying the feat with a mow that would have sent Madame into positive fits. "I am neither rogue nor fool, me. Besides, you have promised to

give me my wedding gown, and to dance in the
round at my marriage fête, Mademoiselle.   But
these are not times to marry.   The linen is for
La Sarte.   She likes nothing so well as linen,
though she has so much of it; it is the way of
the world.   This is her fête-day, and all Faye will
be there.   What say you, Mademoiselle, if I run
down for an hour, and bring you the news?   Life
is become too sad.   We have no fétes now, save to
Madame Liberty; and, my fine, I prefer La Sarte
to Madame Liberty.   I understand La Sarte better
than the other lady; and I believe she can do me
more good, or evil."

"Life is too sad," confirmed Jacqueline, pouting.   "No more royal hunts in royal forests; no
more beautiful plays to be acted with dukes and
duchesses.   And the real stage is republican, representing such anarchy as 'Robert the Robber.'   It
is all too rude.   Neither youth nor age is courted
now.   Men have grown above little cares; and
negligence is the rule, except among dear, noble
old gentlemen like Monsieur my papa.   But there
has been cause; there have been worse things, my

good Babette," Jacqueline corrected herself all at once, looking so exceedingly grave that she went over the boundary line, and became childishly innocent in her awe-struck solemnity. "Do you know that men have eaten bread made of heather, and other poor men have lain eight-and-twenty years in prison without being brought to trial? Eight-and-twenty years! a lifetime. It is quite time,—oh! mon Dieu, it is more than time, that such wrongs were redressed."

"I do not know," answered Babette, a little stolidly; "I never ate bread made of heather, nor anybody in Faye of my acquaintance—only the officer of the king came very often, and salt was dear, and now every one cries 'Peste!' on the paper money, which will be the death of us with arithmetic, if we don't get coin soon. As for lying in prison eight-and-twenty years, I would not have lain eight-and-twenty days, or hours, unless my gaoler had been a were-wolf. Why did men suffer it, Mademoiselle?"

"If the good God suffered it, it might be necessary that men should suffer it too," replied Jacqueline, in a puzzled voice, but with an accent of resignation. The girl was too reverent and too large-hearted to forsake the Divine Figure bending and toiling under the cross in the midst of the rabble rout, on the Dolorous Way, for the human shapes of Socrates and Plato, discoursing abstract-edly in the dignity and retirement of the porch, and even drinking the cup of hemlock juice before a select audience.

A new idea struck Jacqueline: " I will go with you, Babette. La Sarte is a good old woman, and years and virtues ought to be honoured. We are near neighbours, door to door, and Michel is trusted by my father. I also will be at the fête to-night ;" and Jacqueline nodded emphatically.

" Not at all," negatived Babette, with the greatest promptitude and decision ; " the inn is no place for little Mademoiselle."

" But yes," maintained Jacqueline, only spurred by the opposition. " I have gone to the village fêtes before. The dames and demoiselles of the châteaux used to go to all the harvest and vintage

feasts, and to crown the best and prettiest girl.
More than that, we aré all citizens now; and we
ought to love one another. It is a glorious name
that of *citizen*," added the girl, enthusiastically.
"I desire no other."

"Farce !" interjected Babette, incredulously, and
without apology for her bluntness; "so long as you
read and write, and are wise and gentle; and so long
as Solange, for example, spreads manure, plucks
geese, does not know her right hand from her left,
and beats the garçon Louis with a rope, I would
not give the crack of my finger-joints for citizenship, beyond being fellow-creatures—and I suppose
we were that before this hour of the revolutionary
clock. Still you cannot go near La Sarte, Mademoiselle. It is not lucky to go to anybody's fête
empty-handed."

"And I suppose it is too late to make my
purchases from you, my miser? But here I am
already provided;" and Jacqueline drew from her
pocket a little chain of brown hair. "I worked
it, and it seems there is nobody who wants it," she
said, quickly, with a flash of the brown-grey eyes

and a little spasm of the nether lip.   " It is a chain
to give away, and I give it to La Sarte."

" Holy Virgin !   What will La Sarte do with a
hair chain?" persisted Babette, scornfully. " Better
a new halter for one of her cows."

" Keep it among her treasures.   Tie her rosary
to it.   Twist it·round her first grandchild's neck,
with a little relic at the end to preserve him from
harm.   It is to me equal—— But I go, Babette,"
Jacqueline assured her servant, with the roguish air
of a good but very natural little child, who has just
escaped from strict restraint, and vindicates its
lawful freedom.

" Very well, Mademoiselle," acquiesced Babette,
a little sulkily ; " it is true the world is going sense
above, sense below, that is all. When the demoiselles were wont to come from the châteaux to
the fêtes, they were fresh from their convents, and
under the wings of the madames their mothers, as
shy and proud as yon tiresome bird, whose neck
I would ring if I could get at him."

" Babette ! "

" Ah ! well, what business has he to scream

there, and decoy people out for nothing? Those demoiselles danced in their own field with their own partners—lieutenants of the king, commandants, princes. There were three fields,—one for the noblesse, another for the bourgeoisie, and a third for the peasants. Now they are all mixed pêle-mêle. And see what will come of it! Men are so mad to-day, they will throw their sabots over the moon, let alone the mill,—though one woman is as good as another, and better too, to some tastes."

"What is that you say, Babette? I do not understand you;" and Jacqueline turned round with a mystified air.

"You need not ask,"—Babette refused doggedly to explain herself,—"for I will not tell you; and —there, you may fling your tongue to the dogs, Mademoiselle, for you will never guess, never." Babette crossed her arms over her roll of linen, crossed her feet too, and with admirable power of balance, contriving to poise herself on the points of her square shoes, shook herself from side to side in the most approved style of obstinacy. After this pantomime of a sulker, she started afresh with Mademoiselle, through the deserted gate, into the hamlet.

The auberge was the next house in Faye to the Tour. The curé's house — a whitewashed, red-tiled offshoot of the little church, where the willows drooped over the bridge and the brook of the Mousse—was nothing to it; and all the other houses were mere maisonnettes. The auberge was at least half as old as the Tour, and quite as large —in a different fashion. It had never condescended to any sign of its character and capacity, save the line 'Here are lodged man and horse' in faded paint along its front, and the ever wide-open entrance into the court-yard behind. It was known far and near as the Auberge of Faye, and there was no other. The two-storied building was a simple framework of wood, formed in squares, and filled up with mud and plaster — a composition toned by age and mellowed by weather-stains to an umber, or an olive brown. The upper story bulged out, as if seeking space for the overflowing interior, and was propped up by blackened crossbeams. The windows were latticed and oriel. The high-pitched gables were so numerous, and suggestive of so many dormitories, that instead of belonging to the renaissance of Francis I.—as these wooden houses are said to do,—the auberge might have been a forgotten hunting-seat of Dagobert, which had furnished all his knights with separate accommodation, besides supplying stalls for the hunter king's horses and kennels for his hounds.

Doubtless in the palmy days of Faye, when the Tour was so crammed with gracious company that it could hold no more, there had been plumed beavers, gold-laced green coats, sleeves with great knots of riband, appearing and disappearing behind these diamond-paned windows. Now, the sole guests at the auberge were a sous-lieutenant, who had been a shoemaker or a greengrocer in Paris, hurrying with his ragged detachment of brave, wild men to join the French lines, before the Prussian and Austrian forces could reach Lille; a gipsy company from Alsace, looking out for fairs, and bringing dwarfs and giants in their train; a stray member of the gens-d'armes, tying his horse for

an hour to the iron ring in the stone at the
entrance — quite long enough time to excite
general consternation; and a countryman or two.
The gipsy company's caravan and the countryman's waggon had taken the place of the old
family coach with its six or eight horses. And
instead of the turkey stuffed with chestnuts, and
the Chambertin, all the provisions asked for were
soup with plums, eggs with tripe, Gruyère cheese,
brown bread, piquette, and cider.

But the prosperity of the household had not
departed; it had only changed its source and
expression. The old inn had ceased to be a
posting-house save in name, but had become very
much of a great farmhouse. This, indeed, better
suited the requirements of Michel Sart, the innkeeper's elder son, who had bought several lots of
the land Government had to sell, and was also
steward to Citizen Faye. Work-horses and oxen
now occupied the stables; calves and colts were
turned into the herb-garden; sheep, goats, and
pigs trotted into the sheds and ate out of the
mangers and troughs where grooms had washed

panels gilt over with gods and goddesses, and polished silver harness and silver bells. A wooden gallery ran along the back of the auberge half-way up its height, and opened by successive doors into successive gables, cutting them off and rendering them private property. Over this gallery, where formerly long rows of snow-white napery and clothes had hung to dry, and where smart soubrettes had leant down to inspect the court-yard, or exchange lively greetings with the new-comers, there now were spread sheaves of hemp and flax. Only La Sarte herself, and an elderly countrywoman under her, or a staid, heavy farm-servant, clumping about in her wooden shoes, moved here and there, and minded the proper business. Beyond the wooden house itself was the draw-well, in the corner under the cleft elm, with white sand strewn round its mouth, and a rope and bucket dangling. This, and the kennel of the great, gaunt house-dog, Marlbrook, and the swallows' nests in the entrance, were the only things which remained unaltered. Nothing, however, had fallen into decay.

On La Sarte's fête-day every door stood hospitably open; and Marlbrook, complimented with a bone, signalized the holiday by refraining from growling at the numerous company. The audience room was the great chamber of the house,—a long, low apartment, into which every guest, of whatever pretension, had always been shown. The King himself, with his diamond star and his riband of St. Louis, would have been shown there; and for that matter, he was not better lodged in the Tuileries during this summer of fierce mobs; and his fare would be harder still in the Temple. There was a cavernous fireplace, with an equally colossal stove, on which were a mass of bas-reliefs in unpolished iron, being records of strange miracles—St. Roque suspending in mid air his falling mason, St. Hubert transforming his persecutors into stags, and a still more potent saint transforming the devil himself into a grotesque, sprawling flea. Almost as lavishly exuberant and wildly imaginative work was on the great black oak chests which stood opposite Michel's bureau, and where La Sarte

kept her flour and spice, and household linen.
Other works of art—curious old images in wood,
whose subjects extended from " the Tree of Love "
to " the Seven Deadly Sins "—were displayed on
shelves put up for the purpose; and the corner
cupboards were filled with vessels in fayençe, of
the Tours porcelain,. coarse but gay. In a recess
was La Sarte's version of Madame the Baronne's
bed at the Tour, hung with faded tapestry, and
chiefly remarkable for its height; so that if La
Sarte or any ordinary woman had ever occupied
it, she must have mounted to it by means of a
ladder. And she would then have found herself
in nervous closeness to the ceiling, and been
forcibly reminded of La Fontaine's pert critic, with
his reflection on the stalks of pumpkins and the
branches of acorn-bearing oak trees, as well as
the opportune nap and startling accident which
cured him. For La Sarte's ceiling was not bare ;
on the contrary, it was garnished and garlanded
with all sorts of weapons of offence, from which
the tapestry sky of the bed would have afforded
little protection. La Sarte's bed recess was also

her oratory; at the head of which stood her cup with holy water, and the wooden effigy, in miniature, of her patron saint.

Here, where the steam of many a traveller's banquet had gone up into the pure, sunny air, the evidences of good cheer were not wanting. Rich juicy-looking brown hams depended from the ceiling; strings of Normandy pippins, onions, and pilchards were festooned on the walls; a sack with walnuts, and another with chestnuts, stood conveniently near the billets of wood for the stove. Neither had La Sarte failed in providing for the present refreshment of the thronged circle, in the centre of which she sat. The buffet was set out with hot savoury dishes of eels in sailor guise, pigeons with cabbages, partridges with onions; and these were constantly replaced from exhaustless stores about the stove. Then there were rich balls of paste, Neufchâtel cheese, vine leaves of cherries, Medoc of a fair vintage, and a flask of brandy for the little drams.

Each individual as he entered, was invited, after offering his congratulations, to retire to the

buffet and help himself. All Faye was there
—man, woman, and child; but the men rather
preponderated. The gallant Frenchmen did not
fail in their homage, especially when, added to
the claims of politeness, was the important consideration that the aubergiste's elder son, Michel,
was steward at Faye, and the younger, Jonquille
—who not half a dozen years before had been
a flighty fiddler—was now a popular deputy at
Paris, a still greater man than Michel, and with
vast powers of influence and protection in the
eyes of his simple fellow-villagers. Moreover, in
those days of unsettled rule and apprehended
disaster, La Sarte's abundant supper was not to
be despised.

The company consisted of peasants, with the
exception of Michel Sart, who had risen to the
rank of the bourgeois. The men were in holiday costume—grey jackets, long yellow or white
vests, knee breeches, blue and white stockings.
The women had the cap without ribands, and
the warm-toned petticoat and apron, of Babette.
Many of them were young, and exhibited delicate

lace of their own weaving in their caps and stomachers, gold crosses, and silver edging to the seams of their corsages.   This was not merely for their own satisfaction and that of the world at large, but to gratify the grey eyes of Michel Sart, who was a bachelor—a superb party, who had grown up over their heads, and, had it not been for the Revolution, would have been called by every one Maitre Michel, but who gave himself no airs, and was perfectly simple and frank to his old friends. But, as though to include the extreme limits of youth and age in the tribute to La Sarte, both the men and women of the past and the future were around her.   There were octogenarians, leaning on sticks bearing Turks', wolves', or boars' heads, who remembered the *Te Deums* for the victories of the Condé. There were little old women, with merry faces, wrinkled as no gutta percha will wrinkle, who might have been fairy godmothers to fair prin-cesses,—asleep for a hundred years,—and who were ready to lead the cotillons to La Sarte's honour, standing in the same dance with their grandchildren, and acquitting themselves with all the vivacity, if not all the agility, of their teens. And there were little marmots of children, wearing high-crowned caps without borders, long-waisted gowns, or vests, and carrying big bouquets of honeysuckle, roses, jasmine, and myrtle, to commemorate the day. They looked more old-fashioned than their grandsires and grandams.

La Sarte was seated in the centre of the crowd, her son Michel standing behind her, like a sovereign supported by the Crown Prince who is also Prime Minister. She was on a fauteuil, with the gifts of her friends piled about her, at her feet, and on each side :—wool, flax, chickens, a coal-black kitten, eggs, butter, coarse coloured engravings (oftenest of the Virgin and Child), specially blessed rosaries, silk neckerchiefs and handkerchiefs, even chemises, petticoats, and nightcaps. No end to the proofs of La Sarte's mingled supremacy and favour. But the most valuable of all was out of sight. The pretty little white cow, Blanchette, of the rare and valuable breed

La Sarte prized, had cost Michel a secret journey of many leagues, and nearly as many Louis-d'ors, before she stood that day in the neighbouring field, her front legs padlocked together, and a bell round her neck.

La Sarte remained on her throne, and took the homage quietly, though graciously. She was a remarkable person; and so was her son Michel, standing there in the golden glow of the declining sun. Yet mother and son were totally unlike. She had one of those thin, sharp, clear-cut faces which match well with an olive skin. Her eyes, like velvet in their blackness, were benevolent in their open good will; but her mouth was firm to rigidity. The face was that of an upright woman. It was merciful, with wells of tenderness deep down in her nature, but not demonstrative or sympathetic. It was a face austere in its righteousness. Such faces are not infrequent in the country of Calvin, Pascal, and Mère Angelique. La Sarte displayed a scrupulously neat dress, but not finer in quality or different in cut from those which marked the peasant origin of the women around her. Her gown was of dark purple woollen stuff; her neckerchief of blue linen, very pure in the dye and orderly in the folds; and on her head, like many of the older women present, she had a snowy cambric cap without borders, after the fashion of the children, and which, with her brown-black hair removed from her forehead, and concealed under the plain band, exposed her profile, at once strong and fine in its outlines.

Michel Sart was a large, somewhat heavy man for his twenty-six years, with a marked leonine cast of face, and a quantity of tawny hair tied behind in a queue, from a manly, straightforward sense of his rise in rank; a sense equally evident in his riding-coat of olive cloth, fine linen, English long boots, and cocked hat, when he walked abroad. He was an earnest-faced man, with a towering figure, the size and weight of which became him, as his mother's clear profile and brown hue became her. At Faye, Michel was not a hero, like his younger brother; he was that rarer thing, a man who has risen in life without exciting

a tumult of envy and abuse. Perhaps the reason
was that his acquaintances considered him a little
of a boor, and, in spite of his success, called him
sometimes "poor Michel," since he made no fine
speeches, but was shy, and frequently awkward
and brusque. La Sarte, far from being ignorant
and apathetic, like the generality of French
peasants, had taken care that both her sons
should receive a good education ; and Michel
was even a greater scholar than Jonquille, and was
an associate and friend of the curé's. Yet what
did that signify when Michel was no orator,
but withdrew from notice, and was in constant
danger of saying a spade was a spade, with as
little tact and discrimination as the greatest block-
head ? Still Faye had profound confidence in
Michel Sart's judgment and fortune ; and justly.
Scores, fifties, hundreds of such men as he left
the country villages among the five hundred
thousand peasants' sons which Napoleon's wars
cost France, to return with, it might be, strange
vices acquired in their campaigns, but with the
accent and the step of command—self-conceen-

trated, steadfast, and stern—colonels' and gene-
rals' epaulettes on their shoulders, marshals' bâtons
in their hands.

Michel Sart was old, in his class and condition,
to have no wife. But there seemed an appropriateness in this, for it was like Michel to be patient
and contented with his old mother, who had not
chosen a partner for him; to be self-denying and
wise, in letting others be mated, while he stood
aside, looked on, and waited, till the proper hour
and the proper woman came.

La Sarte had named her elder son Michel,
because he was born on the day of St. Michel
and all Angels, and had prayed that he might
be a strong angel to his house and his friends;
just as she had vowed Jonquille from his youth
to the Virgin, and caused him to wear her colours
of blue and white throughout his childhood,
that he might be under the protection of the
blessed among women for the rest of his life.
Who knows how far the names and the prayers
from good and honest hearts fulfilled their design ?

Such was the scene, such the company, at La Sarte's fête. If the card party at the Tour was like a group by Greuze or Watteau, the assembly in the auberge might have given a subject to a French Teniers.

To the full circle, the Citoyenne Jacqueline and Babette, from the Tour, appeared unexpectedly at the open door, when the topics of the day—the chances of the conscription, the convulsions of the struggle between the Aristocrats and the Republicans, the march of the foreign armies —were under lively discussion.

" If the rogues of Austrians come to Faye," cried spirited old Mother Petit, " I will fight them with my distaff and my nails—Go l "

" Eh! well, if I were only a young girl again!" ejaculated a contemporary with poignant regret.

" If you please, Grandmother Huc?" queried a man.

" I would dissemble to catch their hearts, my son, till scores of them drowned themselves and their fine uniforms in the Mousse—as many a a fine fellow at Faye threatened to do for a taste of my lips, my child, before your mother was born."

" But, grandmother, women employ other arms now."

" The more fools they, cadet."

The quaver of the old women's boasting was interrupted by the shrill exultation of another generation. Pacific, taciturn, obese Father Jullien's wife, who was mortally jealous of her husband's fat, being herself lean, gadding, and long-tongued, was describing with much emphasis and relish how Monsieur the President of the Court at La Maille had walked through the whole town at the head of a procession, leading by the hand the President of the Gossips of the Market, as if she were the Austrian woman herself, in order to show that he was a good citizen, win public approbation, and save his property from further ravages. Now why should not Monsieur the Citizen at the Tour be forced to lower his villanous head, and do the Faye gossips the honour to walk with one of them through Faye?

"Where would be the honour, Mother Jullien?" inquired La Sarte, looking into Mother Jullien's heated, grimacing face with her calm, soft, velvet eyes,—the most republican eyes in the room, if republicanism be freedom, not licence. "Which of the two would be the honoured person? Where would be the gain, my heart?"

"There would be this gain, La Sarte," growled Sylvain the butcher, who never addressed anybody except by their bare name: "we who crawled behind yesterday would march before to-day. Bah! better than the escort of the late Monsieur,—let him drive my cart, and let me loll in his coach." Sylvain had not dressed for the gala, but had his soiled, purple-stained apron rolled round his waist. He was a coarse caricature, in his shock head of hair, his saturnine face seamed and scarred, and his Rabelais humour, of Gabriel Mirabeau, who laid the axe at the root of his own order, and whom Maria Theresa's daughter met, under the silent stars and the whispering night breezes, too late to save the monarchy.

"You would not find it an easy seat, Sylvain,"

objected Michel. "Besides, the Citizen uses no coach now; at least we have no horses up yonder at the Tour."

"Hundred devils! The better for the lack of them," shouted and gesticulated irritable little Pepin, who kept the single shop in the hamlet, but had learned to despise the support from the Tour. "We have had horses too long,"—unconsciously identifying himself with the dogs of nobility. "We shall walk on foot at last, and suffer that our neighbours ride. Down with the tyrants! though you have the misfortune to serve one of them, Maitre Michel. Rascals! cowards! crush them! annihilate them!" throwing himself into an attitude of fierce attack, stamping his diminutive foot, and flourishing his shrunk arm.

On the instant of the utterance of these words, the late Demoiselle de Faye and Babette crossed the threshold.

"What is it that you will annihilate, Citizen Pepin?" inquired the little Mademoiselle, pleasantly; "the vipers, the owls?"

Everybody started, and recoiled as if he or she had been one of so many conspirators. The old slavish subservience rushed back on the malcontents. Citizen Pepin wheeled round as on a pivot, placed his hand on the confused wrath of his little heart, and bowed, with his heels together, to the very ground. Mother Jullien cringed, and made as if she would kiss Jacqueline's high-heeled shoe. And while the peasant girls were as fascinated as ever by Mademoiselle's gloves and curled feathers, the old women compared her sweet looks to this or that Dame or Demoiselle de Faye long forgotten in the present world. Only Sylvain the butcher maintained his brutal bearing, and stared at Jacqueline till she winced.

La Sarte and Michel rose, stepped forward, and received the new comers with no more outward show than the frank good will and quiet cordiality with which they had received their other guests. Nevertheless, a vigilant watcher might have remarked that Michel Sart, who was wont to be as immoveable as a rock, flushed scarlet for a moment, while his broad hand on the back of his mother's chair shook like a leaf.

The Citoyenne Jacqueline, who gloried in the name of Citoyenne, came in among the rest of the citizens and citoyennes, as poor, generous, yet vindictive Marie Antoinette strayed in her youth among the cottagers at Trianon. Waving her little white hands, bidding the company be seated, and rest tranquil, Jacqueline looked round her affably and encouragingly, behaving, without the least idea of what she was doing, like a young princess among her vassals.

The guests at La Sarte's fête being French peasants, sometimes stupid, but always adroit in their stupidity, soon accommodated themselves to circumstances, shook off their agitation, and became interested and critical spectators of the Citoyenne Jacqueline's performances.

Jacqueline wished La Sarte many pretty single-hearted good wishes, and presented to her, with infinite grace, the little chain, woven of the brown hair, with the sun shining on it. It was a light

trifle among the offerings there, and yet it was
part of the girl's individuality, being the work
of those hands unused to work, but made, to
judge from their dainty size and shape, for kissing, card-playing, touching the harpsichord, un-
picking gold thread, and—well, thank Heaven!
for praying as much as the most work-hardened
hands present.

La Sarte was not overpowered, but she was
touched. " Thank you, my little lady.   How kind
you are! What fine hair! I hope you have not
robbed yourself," looking at the long thick curls
half way down Jacqueline's back.   " I should not
like that ; but there seems no fear of it.   Touch it,
my Michel ; feel how fine it is."

Michel's face flushed again, and he made a
backward movement, and spoke at first as if he
were about to commit one of his gruff, bashful
blunders. " Pardon. Judge you if I can feel it
with my hand, my old woman?" holding out a great
hand, not browner than any hunter's, but certainly
tanned like leather.   The next moment he proved
that extremes meet : " My hand is too hard.   I

can only feel it thus ;" and the massive, tawny lion's head stooped low over his mother's shoulder till the lips touched the chain.

"Maître Michel is a courtier after all! Go to ; see now the world is turning back again. This is not salutation and fraternity ; this is homage !" was expressed in condemning pantomime by the audience.

Even Babette gave her head a toss, as if she disapproved of the act of gallantry to her mistress's token. Indeed it was a fact that the gayer and more condescending Jacqueline made herself, the tarter and tarter her follower Babette—formerly the life of every village fête— became, until it appeared as if she might have been taking lessons from Madame's woman, her rival and natural enemy, Agathe. There were only La Sarte, Michel, Sylvain the butcher (with his half scowl, half leer), and Jacqueline herself, who took Michel's act as a matter of course. At the same time Jacqueline opened her eyes with a still more meditative speculation in them than before.

"I shall tie my cross to it," decided La Sarte
—"my poor Jonquille's cross, which he forgot
when he went to Paris," she added in an un-
dertone; "and then I will remember you in my
prayers."

"Do so, my mother," said Jacqueline, gratefully
and humbly; "and I will remember you, and
Michel, and Jonquille;—only Michel, who is the
friend of the curé, has more need to remember a
naughty girl like me;" and she darted a quick look
at Michel, who bent his head in acknowledgment
of her words, but said nothing.

Sylvain the butcher articulated hoarsely, "Yes,
there!" gave an ugly grin, and then sighed
in so profound a manner that the whole company looked at him,—an attention which caused
him immediately to laugh loudly and make a
profane speech. La Sarte, in her turn, spoke
to Sylvain a word of grieved, but honest and
long-suffering reproof, and the evening's entertainment went on.

Jacqueline ate a bit of a galette and a few
cherries, put a glass to her lips to the health of

La Sarte particularly and the company generally, and then sat down amongst the other citizens,—in the place of honour, it must be told,
next La Sarte, fully prepared to join in the
diversions.

There were pipes and a player ready for rondes,
to please both old and young; but the amusements began with games, and the first—again
after an old custom, better left in disuse at this
time—was led by Mademoiselle.

She initiated the circle in "the Garden of my
Aunt," saying in her bell-like voice, while her
manner, in its utter unconsciousness, was the
most perfect manner in the world, "I have
just come from my aunt's garden. What a
beautiful garden, my aunt's garden! In my
aunt's garden there are four corners," nodding
eagerly to each member of the party who
played, as he or she repeated her phrases in
thick patois :—

"In the first corner
Is found a jasmine."
"I love you without end."

("Say that, Jeanneton.") Then directing a second
player to follow with the second verse,—

> "In the second corner
>   Is found a rose."
> "I would like much to embrace you,
>   But I dare not."

(" Charming ! Philippe.")   Still advancing with
the game,—

> "In the third corner
>   Is found a beautiful pink."
> " Tell me your secret."

Then, in the character of mistress of the cere-
monies, Jacqueline addressed the entire room,—
" Come, let each say to each his little secret, quite
low ;" and she inclined her head with an unhesi-
tating charm, to receive the whisper of the registrar
Michel. After everybody had copied her sovereign
example, Jacqueline held aloft and flourished, like
a cobweb in the sunshine, the flimsy snare in the
eyes of the players. She recited in glee and
triumph the fourth and concluding verse,—

"In the fourth corner
  I found a handsome poppy."
"What you have said quite low
  Repeat quite loud."

And every ignorant whisperer felt like a be-trayed, guilty man or woman as he or she had to proclaim audibly—abashed by the silliness of the sentence—the private communication to the next neighbour.

By rights the gallantly-frivolous French game induces gallant, fantastically-appropriate whispers. One would be a butterfly or a little bird on the jasmine or the pink ; another would shed the rose leaves at a beloved friend's feet. But the heavy peasants of Faye knew nothing of those fine speeches which the working men and women of Paris could have exchanged glibly at the most horrible junctures. Their whispers were of such gross, tangible human affairs as " What dost thou think of that for a fine breast-knot, Mar-got ? " " Wilt thou be at the mass on Sunday, Etienne ? " " Hast thou seen my brown mare, Claude ? " " What number wilt thou choose for

the drawing?"—varied by such home thrusts
as "What hast thou done to big Jean, my fine
girl?" and Babette's sarcastic address to Citizen
Pepin, "Will the red cap give thee a beard,
my master?" alluding to that important addition to a man's attractions, the few hairs on
the sallow, pointed chin, which the small shop-
keeper would have cherished dotingly, and whose
absence he was understood to regret bitterly.

Sylvain had constructed his whisper into a
shallow, hideous riddle: "What lady will soon
be alone in France, and wear the brightest crimson?"

Jacqueline had declared, quite naïvely and
earnestly, "My secret is, 'There is a drop of
dew like a pearl falls right down from heaven
every night on the hedge-roses, and the mosses
on the thatched roofs.' I would I could catch
such a drop of dew," she continued, wistfully;
"but the roses of the Tour are so surrounded
with thickets, and its stone roof is so thick."

La Sarte, with the quick intuition of her
younger son, the genius in the double-entendre,

and with her own long look forward over all the heads, explained, "For me, I said, 'If it is necessary that I be a flower, I hope I may be a sweet-smelling sprig of lavender or rosemary, to scent all the rooms in the auberge, and in Faye, if it were possible, a long time after I shall be transplanted into God's garden.' That would be better worth than to be a crown of immortelle or a cross there."

As for Maitre Michel, he was more literal and prosaic than any of them. He had taken the opportunity of impressing on his old lord's daughter, "You will not walk alone with Babette after sunset, my Mademoiselle; I shall accompany you to the Tour."

"Mademoiselle, indeed!" muttered Mother Jullien through her teeth, and sniffed the air with her knife-like nose, "I thought the titles were swept away with the flood!" In spite of this, however, she was ready to throw herself in Jacqueline's way as she passed to the door, and tried to catch her eye as she whined and fawned her good night; for there were still stores dispensed in the village from the Tour kitchen, impoverished as it was. And who knew but some fine day the titles might be restored, and the Sieurs be as awful as ever? It were best to be square with everything. And indeed, it was all left for her to do, for that ton of flesh, Father Jullien, would not stir, except to take in more meat and drink into his greasy carcase.

Jacqueline, in her double rôle of citoyenne and princess,—always unaware that she was playing a part, or doing anything unusual on the clay floor of the village inn,—curtseyed with the low, soft, inclusive curtsey of the exploded régime, smiled blandly, and accepted Maitre Michel's escort as simply in the way of his duty.

Babette walked behind her young lady and the registrar,—not sniffing, spiteful, and Janus-faced, like Mother Jullien, for Babette was a greater creature altogether, and scorned and hated the other's meanness and malice,—but cold and stiff with mortification and rage, and making no cere- mony in her mental record of her feelings.

The nightingale was still singing its passion in

the bocage, and the evening star was shining out over the terrace. Madame and Monsieur had not left off their cards in the hot, heavily perfumed boudoir; or their strongly spiced State and Court scandal; or their elegant follies and cynicisms. Their young daughter was walking the hundred yards with the retainer, by whose side she needed no chaperon, flushed with the honest, ingenuous, warm-hearted pleasure of conferring pleasure; and with a secret, undefined fluttering wonder at her servant's devotion.

Maître Michel, strong, staid, simple, and un-polished, was as chivalrous to her as if he had been a squire of the middle ages, attending on one of the early Demoiselles de Faye. He was just as if there was no turbulent Convention in Paris, of which his brother was a deputy of note; no Jacobin and Cordelier clubs ruling the great kingdom of France, and fiercely snatching the plumed hats from the nobles' heads, — nay, threatening to cut off the heads themselves as the mower's scythe crops the tiny clover heads in the meadow grass. Maître Michel reverenced

the ground Jacqueline trod on, noted down every
look and word of hers, treasured them up, and
brought them out of his long, deep memory
every time he could give her a moment's pleasure.   She did not know how she had found it
out, but she was as sure that Maitre Michel was
her most faithful servant, as that the future head
of the house of Faye, Achille René, Chevalier
de Faye, her splendid young cousin, had been
drawn presumptively from the ranks of bachelor-
hood (to which all chevaliers as well as abbés were
wont to be reduced) and was decreed to be her
betrothed bridegroom.   She knew, too, that the
consciousness of Michel Sart's lavish, unselfish service—though she could not render any further
explanation of it than that Michel was old-
fashioned and loyal, a watch-dog and a lion to
the house of Faye—soothed her and gratified her,
although she had only a dim half-appreciation of
its worth, and was puzzled to sound its depth.
At the same time Achille de Faye's fitful atten-
tions, his long absences, his flying visits, and the
perilous uncertainty of their connection in those

times, filled her with strange chagrin, which she dared not show. Jacqueline was therefore under a happy influence as she walked up the sandy street to the conciergerie of the Tour. She kept prattling to her big guardian, and telling him confidentially, " They are dear, good country people, Maitre Michel,—honest people. I am very glad I came among them. I love them all. Ah! well!" correcting herself, — " except that Sylvain the butcher, who makes my skin feel like a hen's skin. He is as—as one of the satyrs I have read of in the classics. I think,"— she pressed nearer her stout servant,—" I think he smells of blood."

"I don't know, Mademoiselle, that Sylvain is cruel for a butcher," Michel checked her gently. "I believe he would spare a beast to suit a fancy; though I have heard say he chose his trade after he was a man, to learn how killing felt for an occupation."

" Mother Jullien is not sincere. I know she is angry against me because I was Demoiselle before I was Citoyenne. That was not my fault. Yet without doubt these two poor people have had their trials, of which I comprehend nothing,—I, who am a little fool of idleness and luxury. But let us return to our sheep: your mother is a good angel, Maitre Michel."

"She is a good old woman, Mademoiselle," answered Michel, temperately; "there is not a better old woman in France."

"That is a true truth, Maître Michel," Jacqueline assured him sententiously; "but do not call *me* Mademoiselle, when it is no longer the usage,—when we are going back to simple, grand, primitive times—fresh, beautiful times. I—I obey the laws. I wish the poor people who have been oppressed to be free and happy. I am content, proud, to be called Citoyenne Jacqueline; though many demoiselles, who are no better taught, detest and despise the term.". And Jacqueline, modestly sensible of her superiority, threw back her curls with a stately motion.

"Very well, Citoyenne Jacqueline," Michel Sart humoured her, with a little half-formed, pensive smile about his kind mouth, the lines of which made him look old and tried in the vigour of his prime; "and you will no longer call me Maitre Michel."

"That is quite another thing," objected Jacqueline, thoughtlessly. And the moment the words passed her lips, she had a perception, bred of the complete code of politeness in which she was reared, that she had been insolent. She would far sooner have insulted an equal; she would almost as soon have struck Babette. A French noble must have far forgotten herself, when she taunted a man of the people, though ever so lightly, with his inferiority of degree. She flushed scarlet all over her throat and forehead, and hurried to efface the affront by the softest, most caressing words and images she could summon on the emergency.

"You love your mother, Michel Sart." She said the name deliberately. "She has a good son."

"Thank you, Mademoiselle,—Citoyenne," Michel corrected himself, accepting the propitiation quietly. "There is no merit in being a good son to a good mother, who loved me first, though not best."

"What do you say?" questioned Jacqueline, inquisitively, recovering from her shame and contrition.

"My brother Jonquille is La Sarte's favourite son," declared Michel.

"No," negatived the girl incredulously, in surprise at the decided statement. "Jonquille is a little more famous than when he came up to the Tour, to play his violin before my music master. Behold the scene:— Monsieur Cars is wicked, and sneezes as he takes snuff; Jonquille breaks his violin in a rage,—you remember, Maître Michel? you pick up the fragments, and say politely, 'No, I thank you,' for your brother, when Monsieur has remorse, fear — I do not know what — and pretends to be generous, and offers Jonquille one of his squeaking, cracked old violins. But La Sarte is not a mere villager—she will not worship her younger son because he is a deputy. Faith of Faye! she has no need. There are vile deputies, as there are noble—noble in heart I mean, not alone in name. The five wise and the five foolish virgins, is it not so? I pray there may not be more than five foolish, as Monsieur my father no longer doubts—— But Jonquille is not foolish ; only he is not so wise as you, Maitre Michel, with all his cleverness. Let La Sarte see to it," Jacqueline maintained, a little indignantly.

" Pardon, Mademoiselle." Both of them, in spite of private opinion and private enthusiasm, tacitly returned to the old names. " How noble tongues go! My mother prefers Jonquille, not because he is a deputy, but because he best merits and repays her love."

" Do you mean it ? "

" Yes," he asserted in his cool manliness. " Why should I not mean it, when it is the truth? and why should I say it if I did not believe it ? "

" Why, truly? And you would die for your mother, Maître Michel ? "

" I hope so, if God bade me," he replied, gravely. " He would give me the strength, and it would be my privilege as well as my duty."

" I believe it, I believe it ! " cried Jacqueline,

with a full heart. "I believe you would even die
for us at the Tour,"—in a more breathless voice,
and with a still more dewy moisture in the brown-
grey eyes,—"for me, good Michel."

"Ah! that would be my happiness, my glory,"
broke from the sober Michel, with a ring in his
calm voice, and a flash from his reasonable eyes.
And then silence descended upon the speakers—
only broken by the rich, sweet yearning plaint of
the nightingale up in the bocage.

Babette stalked behind the couple fuming and
fretting inwardly: "Very good, Maitre Michel.
You advance, my brave boy! you used to be so
modest, you could not embrace a girl after she had
danced the bourrée with you,—save like a little boy
full of bashfulness, holding the tips of her fingers,
and just coming nose against nose;—that was all.
Now you kiss Mademoiselle's chain, and you walk
by her side to the Tour; and I and my little web of
linen are worth nothing. Bah! I have found you
out—it was not the false shame, but the pride.
You are as proud as Lucifer, my good man; and
you prefer to look up to a star, and die or run mad

with the longing, to mating with an honest girl
your equal. Ouf! what asses and mules are these
great, wise, good fellows! Don't you see, then,
that she has no more thought of you, save as her
humble servant the registrar, than of a horse or a
dog? Little coquette, trifler, actress that she is!
—a baby who does not know enough of harm to
intend harm, so that I cannot punish her. She
walks with you, dolt, because a registrar is not a
man. Do you think, dupe, she would walk thus
with the Chevalier her lover, her future husband;
or that Madame would permit it, or ever have her
lynx eye off the child? For me, I do not know
whether I could cry like a watering-pot or scratch
somebody's eyes out. But Mademoiselle, though she
is conceited, vain, meddlesome, will have enough of
troubles of her own,—poor little angel, our Lady
aid her! She is as vain as a peacock; and she
has the rage of a fiery, aristocratic sparrowhawk.
What does she want with a tame, common thrush
in addition to the other sparrowhawk? But then
she is noble to the core. If any one suffers she

flies to the rescue, though she should suffer instead. She is brave, daring. Clever though she be, she would no more suspect you of deceiving and abusing her, though you did it under her nose, than of your proposing to strangle her—the darling ! No, Maitre Michel, it is you who are to be blamed ; you are a great, wise, brave, rich, kind, humble, proud monster. Go ! you are not worth a virtuous, sensible girl's regard, if it were not that you would ruin yourself among these aristocrats without her."

After the last extraordinary jumble of epithets, Babette surreptitiously shook her fist. It was a powerful fist for a woman,—one that could have caught up a fellow like Citizen Pepin (suspected of having a sneaking kindness for the waiting woman) by the high collar, and half shaken the breath from his attenuated body. There was modest reticence and a sort of extravagant womanly honour in Babette's unrequited devotion to a giant of a registrar—a man of the physical calibre of Maitre Michel.

The gate was gained; a bow and a·curtsey, a snappish nod and a cordially-indifferent good evening, exchanged; and the ill-assorted company separated.

CHAPTER III.

 FEW weeks later in the summer the village of Faye was dark in its verdure; the walnuts were as big as blackbirds' eggs; the bunches of grapes had lost their faint blue and green, and were deepening into plum colour, or blanching into straw colour, on the cottage trellises. The Tour de Faye was looking more like a lichen than ever, gaunt and grey with golden patches.

Down the hamlet street walked Jacqueline de Faye, in her "mules à talons"—freely translated, Cinderella slippers—with heels which touched the earth lightly. Her train of brocade gently swayed behind her, not dragging on the chaussée, but drawn up in an artistic bunch, like the tail of a symmetrical little bird; a long-waisted, close-fitting corsage covered her beautifully shaped bust; clouds of lace hung from her round arms; while a soft, transparent lace mob-cap rested on her flowing hair, and came across by the ears.

Leading Jacqueline by the hand was her kinsman and elected bridegroom, the young noble, the Chevalier de Faye,—himself a sight gallant and brave, though his fine feathers had been clipped. Instead of the old velvet and taffetas, he now wore no finer stuff than cloth, like Maitre Michel. Like Maitre Michel, too, his coat took the form of a redingote, loose as a sack, with long tails, huge collar, and epaulettes turned back the breadth of the chest. He had a plain cravat tied in a big bow; boots à la hussard; his cocked hat on his head instead of under his arm; and his disengaged hand in his coat pocket, à la Englishman or American. The

change was significant.   The advancing Revolution had only spared the Chevalier one high-
bred distinction besides his birth and bearing,
and that was his long dark hair, which, though
free from powder, was perfumed, and partly tied
in a queue, partly arranged in side locks, so as
to fall curling at the ends to the shoulders, in
what were then called Dogs' Ears, which were
so esteemed that they were only cut off, or
plaited and turned aside, when the. dandy head
was laid at rest on the block.   The face within
the frame of hair was languid and a little super-
cilious in expression; the mouth was turned down
at the corners; the well-moulded and slightly
projecting chin was turned up to approach the
nose, which was broadish and inclined to flat-
ness; the eyes were long and liquid, but not fully
opened; and the complexion was a good bronze.
To most people it was a noble, comely counte-
nance enough, but pleasure-loving and sensual,
though not without intellect; fond of change,
though contented; and quite capable of a

sneer. Notwithstanding his being stripped of his old splendour, the Chevalier was a wonderful young fop, who—supposing he survived the times—might one day rise up a hero.

It would have been comparatively easy for a woman to resist the Chevalier in his old velvet and gold, when he, like the rest of the nobles, had no higher ambition than to embroider at women's frames in women's saloons,—lower Herculeses, since their Omphales had not imposed upon them the effeminate tasks,—or to stroll in the gardens of the Tuileries or the galleries of Versailles, pulling the strings which set the imbecile cardboard toys—the pantins—in wriggling motion. The only manliness that was ever heard of in them was their baptism of fire in the wars; their brutal adventures in the little houses near Paris; their gambling away of soul and body at the receptions of marchionesses and duchesses; their bloody duels at Longchamps.

But now, in the gathering gloom of adversity,

it was not so easy for some natures to resist the
young men heretofore nobles.

Madame de Pompadour's favourite phrase,
" After us, the Deluge," was in the act of fulfilment.   The early waves had broken over the
high heads, but they were dauntless and dignified
as ever ; while the hard, selfish hearts were learn-
ing strange lessons of sympathy and feeling in
the midst of vanity and destruction.   Boys of
one or two-and-twenty were, in a few months,
growing resolute, devoted men in that hotbed of
Paris, where a moral volcano had rent and
scattered all the old elements.

The first wave of Madame de Pompadour's
deluge—the wave of Jean Jacques' sentimental
brotherhood ; the farce of beggars standing as god-
fathers to children of men of letters, who wrote in
ruffles, with genealogical trees hanging over their
heads ; the furor for Benjamin Franklin—had rolled
by unnoticed.

The second wave—noblemen constituting themselves tradesmen, in order that they might sit

in the Third Estate; rising and thundering against their own order, and turning and biting their own flesh and blood; detachments of soldiers from every branch of the service, drinking and huzzaing with the mob; trees of liberty; Phrygian red caps; oaths to the Constitution; beautiful women of degree making appointments among the ruins of the Bastille; nuns driven abroad all over the country, blinking at the hot, broad sunshine; women of the market insulting Marie Antoinette, while the aquiline nose and the Austrian lip came out, as under a livid light and against a dark background, more prominently than before;—the waters of that formidable wave too had broken and dispersed, doing little more than foam up mire and dirt.

But more terrible waves were at hand,—waves which brought shoals of gleaming pikes, blood pattering from them like rain; the guillotine, a ghastly phantom before and after and for all time in the Square du Carrousel,—the Square

of Louis Quinze, the Square of the Revolution, the Square of Peace (what will be the
next title?); everywhere a crowd of unclean,
fierce, impious, shrieking demons, as if the mad
blasphemy of "Long live hell!" had been heard
in high Heaven, and the Pit had yawned open,
and let loose its damned crew on accursed France.
Within forty days of Louis XV.'s death, Jean of
Beauvais had preached a Lent sermon to the
Court on the text, "Yet forty days, and Nineveh
shall be overthrown!" And Nineveh was falling.

Jacqueline and her kinsman walked down
the hamlet street on the very eve of the day
when dull, gentle, proud Louis, after having
subscribed the "Rights of Man," stood three
miserable hours with his wife and children,
besieged and bullied in his palace by the scum
of the faubourgs; put on the red cap where the
crown had been; and tore it from his head when
the ordeal was over, screaming, "Madame, did you
come from Vienna to behold me thus degraded?"
None save the Queen, — "the stranger," —
hoped for the intervention of strangers, which

would arouse in Paris the din of a hundred thousand forges. She looked at the moon, and said, "When, in a month, this moon will appear again, I shall be free and happy." Already men like the Chevalier could not walk abroad safely in the streets of the capital and the larger towns, but were forced to daub their clothes, soil their hands and faces, pull coarse shaggy jackets over their coats, and echo the sentiments of the *Ça ira* and the *Marseillaise* at every gathering and stoppage, at the corners of the streets, and before the bakers' shops, or else become victims to the long pent up and now wildly bursting storm of a people's vengeance. Thinking of this, and looking at the young, handsome, smiling man who would smile when he could not pray in the tumbril, it was difficult for any one not to yearn over the sunshiny face,— not to think how short a time had elapsed since the curled head was leant in childish confidence and security against a mother's knee, and was nestled in her bosom,—not to feel how inexperienced he was (whatever follies he had known) in the great mysteries of life and death,—not to fancy that he who could be firm in death would be faithful in life and love.

What did it matter that these workings of the mind were but filmy threads spinning themselves from the young nobleman's rank, beauty, and danger; and that just as certainly as the old Monsieur de Faye, in his speculativeness, and mild contempt for women, showed a nature leavened with the eccentric, half-sweet sourness of Montaigne; so the young Monsieur—worldly, sensual, callous —had a heart and soul leavened with the bitter yeast of Rochefoucauld, although, at the same time, he loved France, glory, fair women, galloping horses, waving feathers, like the son of the people, Joachim Murat?

Jacqueline was not a sorceress. She did not see more of the young noble who led her along the village street, than his pleasant, picturesque exterior, and the imminency of his peril. Before his arrival, she had often plucked at the tie of betrothal which bound them together, was galled by it, and felt tempted to rebel against it, in her

new, half-chivalrous idea of independence, and
of disinterested, divine passion. But now her
rebellion was quelled. It would be base to
break the bond and desert her kinsman in his
misfortunes. By the side of Achille, Jacqueline yielded to natural fascination. She kept
glancing up at her lover, shyly but willingly,
drinking in at every look long draughts of girlish
worship.

Women in France had become less heroic on
their own account since the days of the Pré-
cieuses, even though they were now amateur
republicans. They no longer kept portraits of
Gustavus Adolphus and the Condé hanging in
their chambers ; no longer vowed to them alle-
giance, or declared they would belong to none
less renowned. They no longer needed costly
garlands of Julia, with vignettes and madrigals
by the greatest artists and poets of a bom-
bastic generation, or the gracious intercession
of potent princesses, to bring them down from
the clouds to the suits of honest and gallant men. They no longer called themselves

Sapphos, or their poor small-pox-seamed, war-
worn Pélissons, any fine name that struck their
errant fancies. The greater gain to the men,
if the women were altogether losers by the
change.

Whether Babette was right or wrong in thinking that Madame would never relax the bonds of
etiquette, or so far forget the proprieties as to send
Jacqueline to walk with her promised bridegroom,
here were the two together without premeditation.
The Chevalier had arrived the preceding evening
without warning (there being small space for
warning in those days), had breakfasted alone with
Monsieur, and afterwards, by chance, encountered
Jacqueline doing an errand with Babette in the
village. The lover and his mistress had flown
to each other like fire and tow; and Babette
looked as proud of the accident as if she had
been its author,—as proud as if she were a
mother hen clucking noisily to a favourite chicken
over a new-found grain of corn. Babette, in her
lace cap, golden-brown gown, crimson apron, and
clattering sabots, bridled for her mistress, and

bounced for herself, in turn. She did the next thing to calling the whole world to witness the spectacle. She turned up the whites of her eyes; annihilated her forehead; protruded her chin in a peak; swung her substantial but supple body from side to side; and challenged her acquaintances to remark the pair — not only by the multitude of her becks and wreathed smiles, but by actually hailing them on the steps, in the doorways, at the fountain; using her shrill voice in such significant congratulations as "What a fine day, Balfe!" "What delights in full air, Madeleine! Ah, I love to see the happy people. The grapes will ripen as they have not done since we invented the Nation."

A very different Babette was she from the sullen woman who tramped along, secretly croaking a protest and a denunciation against little Mademoiselle and Maitre Michel, as they walked from the auberge to the Tour on the evening of La Sarte's fête.

The peasants of Faye, notwithstanding their

smitten attachment to that rather troublesome
invention of young France, the Nation, could not
deny themselves so pretty a glimpse of high life,
blooming still in its wreck; and they were almost
drawn back for a moment into the old, blind
adoration of the nobles.   Little Citizen Pepin
leaped to the door of his shop at the sound of
Babette's tongue; and though he started back
somewhat when he saw by whom she was accompanied, he yet removed his casquette with the
slow, reluctant movement of a man uncovering
under the influence of a spell, and stood, grinning
and gaping, and peering out, with a sheepish,
incensed admiration, at the young aristocrats.
But when the cavalcade was out of sight, he soon
recovered himself, to rave and storm at the serpent's and the wolf's brood.   Others than Citizen
Pepin — not creatures of Babette—were moved
to the centre of their impressionable, impulsive
French natures; while the old men and women
shaded their eyes, crossed themselves, and were
so happy that they cried.   It was so like the
fine old times when they were young and poor,

—Sacristie! they were very poor and oppressed, but there were grand lords and ladies walking over them, who were beautiful as angels, and filled one's eyes and roused one's brain better than snuff.

There was a universality in the charm, for did not high and low rush both to the Tuileries and to Kensington Gardens to see Madame Recamier, when she walked on the common grass, in the common sunshine? And then there was only one *rara avis;* but here there were two,—both varieties of the bird.

Maitre Michel saw this last glorious display of the quality; went and worked like a horse for the rest of the day,—measuring, summing up, paying wages, repairing dilapidations with his own hands on Monsieur's domain; and returned at nightfall to the auberge, tired like a dog, as he well might be. He sat drooping in the gallery at the back of the house, where he could see, as through a telescope, under the arched doorway and over a thatch roof, one girouette of the Tour and a corner of the

terrace; and where he could listen to the nightingale, which sang again of love and death in the
bocage. His mother came out and looked at
him with her serene velvet eyes. "You work
too much, my little son," she said to the great
man. "It is necessary that you rest, though
you are strong as a lion. I wish you had a
young wife to say to you, by her looks, 'Rest,
be gay, Michel.'"

"My old wife," replied Michel, with an effort
at pleasantry, and with the fond reverence which
Frenchmen above all men in the world preserve
for their mothers, and which good Catholics in
other quarters of Christendom bestow on the
Madonna, "I am content; I want no young
wife."

Michel little thought how soon a young wife
would sit by his side in that gallery.

To return to the lovers. A shadow fell across
their path in the noonday street. It was that of
Sylvain the butcher, with his dingy repulsive apron,
tucked sash-fashion about his middle, as usual,
and this time with the weapon of his craft—

a huge, ugly cleaver — poised on his brawny
arm. He was tickled, perhaps tormented (for a
miserable as well as horrible man was Sylvain),
but he was not won, by the proximity of the Demoiselle and the Chevalier. He came forward and
made an uncouthly grotesque bow, and flourished
his axe.

"Bon jour. Our masters, still our masters, as
I see. What news from Paris? How flourishes
my brother in trade, Monsieur Paris, and his fine
family? Is he still required to do his work in a
gold-laced coat, white silk stockings, and pumps?
Plenty of work too, eh?" And he felt the edge
of his cleaver.

"Back, canaille!" cried Achille, with an out-
break of fiery scorn. "No insolence from
such a knave as thou. At least I am master
in Faye yet awhile; on the pavé of a hamlet
there is not a thousand animals against one
man."

Sylvain did not give way, but he suffered the
couple to pass him, grinning with a cool superiority that made the blood boil.

"I know the villain," asserted the Chevalier, preventing Jacqueline's explanation. "I have seen him before, and I do not know why, but he forces me to detest him, far below the notice of a gentleman as he is;" and he knitted his arched brows in vexation and spite. "He makes me hot and cold, like a bad omen. I tell you this, my beautiful: if I have a star of destiny and that man has another, my star grows livid and wan when his crosses it,—I am sure of that." He ended with the strain of superstitious fatalism which always attends on an infidel age.

But there were fitter topics of conversation between plighted youth and maid than bad omens, or even stars of destiny. The Chevalier Achille led Jacqueline—followed by Babette at a respectful distance — back to the Tour by the ravine of plum, acacia, and beech treês, which led from the end of the village into the mall. There, under the clear blue sky, in the chequered shade, the verdure, and the seclusion, the two, with their satellite, strayed or sat upon the mossy bank. The violets were all gone, but the tall, purple foxgloves, the slender, pale harebells (which the French call the nuns of the fields), the little scarlet strawberries, and the truffles beneath the beech trees, had taken their place. Still, the Chevalier and Mademoiselle were the brightest flowers. The two talked as became their years and prospects, while Babette drew forth a convenient piece of knitting from her pocket, clicked her needles industriously, and nodded her head so often and with such fervour, that the milky pillar of her throat seemed no more than sufficient to support it.

The Chevalier told Mademoiselle that he could not join the princes and the army of the Rhine, because he could not fight against Frenchmen, sans-culottes though they might be, or fraternize with aliens to invade his native country ; no, not even on the pretext of restoring the monarchy and the *haute noblesse.* Jacqueline listened intently, and thought these sentiments very generous. If she did not liken her young Achille to the great Achilles (the French of the epoch were well up in the classics), nor think that the army of the frontiers, like the host of Greece, would be lost without his single redoubtable arm, she at least believed in his patriotism and self-sacrifice, and, woman-like, pressed nearer to him, rendering simple neutrality more difficult. However, Achille had hopes and intentions which, by lying in close obscurity at Faye, he might be able to fulfil. Trusting that the worst blast of the revolutionary storm had blown over, and knowing emigration, too long deferred, to be now doubly hard to accomplish, he hinted at another and a more satisfactory end to the troubles—the end which had been contemplated before the troubles began. This was the fulfilment of his engagement to Jacqueline, and his living quietly with the family at Faye (his own father and mother being dead) until the kingdom should be restored to peace, right rule, and just supremacy.

"Why should I go away again, my altogether beautiful? I always thought there was much at Faye, but since I came this time, I think there is everything. If you could only suffer me always, Jacqueline, I would be your most humble servant; I am grown humble, I ask no more, my friend."

The Chevalier only thus hinted his desire, because to express it plainly—nay, even to insinuate it to Jacqueline in the first place, as he had just done—was so glaring a departure from French precedent, that her fresh cheeks were dyed a shy modest rose, and her moorland-hued eyes completely veiled. Notwithstanding, the girl forgave the offence the moment it was committed; and the young man, cool enough and skilful enough to note every step of his progress, had no reason to be dissatisfied with his success. Then he relieved his young bride's blushes and perturbation by gliding easily from personal to general topics, and entertaining her with a more enlarged circle of principles and actions. Not those of the political clubs and tribunes, which struck him as out of her way, poor little girl! Nor did he speak of the Assemblies, which no person of distinction above the bourgeoisie dared to frequent, unless under the protection of a powerful Jacobin name. For now the carriage of Fouquier Tinville, public prosecutor, was the only carriage which presumed to roll freely through the crowded, narrow streets where the reckless driving of the coachmen of the nobles had once been a scandal and a by-word, and where listening ears detected beforehand the echo of wheels whose hollow rumble would be the sign of the ghastly banquet of Até and Hecate. No ; Achille descanted on the theatres and the operas, the only amusements left to the French since they had, as Babette said, invented the Nation. He described Glück's "Iphigénie," and "Charles the Ninth," and the débuts of Talma and Mademoiselle Mars, to a girl who had never been in any but provincial theatres, or seen other than strolling stars, and who knew a great deal less of dramatic representation than the old demoiselles of St. Cyr. And when he saw the effect he produced, his excitable French fluency rose to eloquence. He had some taste for poetry, this fine young Monsieur, so he proceeded to spout as well as to describe, with second-hand grace and talent, and that gift of imitation which is alike the strength and the snare of the Gallic races. He was the

Cid, he was Heracleus, he was Titus; until Babette
dropped her knitting needles, and threw up her
hands in admiration of Monsieur the Chevalier's
declamation. Of course she knew no more of
Corneille and his brother poets than of so many
dancing dervishes, and with her rampant common
sense would have mercilessly travestied their
heroics, had she understood them; but she admired the sound of the words a thousand times
more for not understanding their spirit. As
for Jacqueline, she listened like a dear little
country girl, with an unclaimed fund of reverence,
admiration, and love, ready to honour all draughts.
From thinking Achille's opinions chivalrous and
manly she hurried on, with the swiftness of lightning, to set him down as great, even divine; to
bow before him like an eastern princess, sun
herself in his light, shrink in his shadow, tremble
or rejoice at his glance. But she was not so
dazzled or weak-minded either, under this mighty
power which had taken hold of her, that her
faculties could not play. On the contrary, with
the strong awakening influence of sympathy, and

as iron sharpens iron, Jacqueline's nature began
to blossom over and perfume the air, and to
answer to her cousin's courtship by yielding to
him its best—and that was very choice—in return
for his gallant but formal, hackneyed efforts.
Like a royal, imprudent merchant, Jacqueline
bartered good gold with Achille de Faye for
what was no more than highly polished pinch-
beck.

Jacqueline was large-hearted, pure, tender, winning, as she began in her gentle agitation to
speak of her hopes and fears,—not for herself and
her family alone, but for her country and her
kind; to breathe her dim aspirations, which to
this man were a thousand times dimmer; to
chatter of her pets, and amuse him with her
rusticities. He was not like her, he could not
abide sacred homeliness; but—one symptom of
the corruption of the age—he was enamoured of
artificial simplicity.

She gave the Chevalier, in return for his quota-
tions, a quaintly hyperbolical song, Babette beating time with her foot against the trunk of a tree,

and humming the refrain heartily. And while Jacqueline sang, her sweet voice quivered a little from nervousness at Monsieur's great connois-seurship, and from confusion at the looks which now loved more and more to rest upon her, and became more and more fixed and ardent after their first languid glances :—

" Ifi the king had given me
Paris his great city,
And it had been necessary for me to quit
The love of my dear,
I would say to King Henry,
Take back again your Paris,
I love better my dear, O gué!
I love better my dear."

Shyly withdrawing from her lover's compli-ments and allusions, the name of Henry recalled to her the lament for the son of Henry which the journal of the Feuillants, the *Acts of the Apostles*, had just dared to publish in Paris;—which, with its mournfully cadenced fall, continually repeated,—

" Louis the son of Henry
Is a prisoner in Paris."

The all-loyal, half-republican girl could only sing of Monsieur Capet under her breath, even in the Ravine of the Plum-trees at Faye, with a face grown grave and timid, as it turned a look of love to Achille, the future head of the family, with his tenfold accountability and danger.

Babette hummed no refrain to this doleful ditty, but shook her head in decided reprobation : " For me, I will not waste my breath on the melancholy. And what good would it do the King in Paris if I were to lose my head here at Faye? My head would be very little to him, but it is something — and a good deal, too — to me. Miséricorde ! these aristocrats, the very best of them, are fools."

The Chevalier being an aristocrat naturally judged otherwise. Listening to the abiding sentiments of royalty and honour, the religion of his class,—piety and the doctrine of the divine right of kings and rulers being in many minds, at many eras, inseparable,—and remembering the gracious words of sympathy and hope which the girl had already spoken for the mistaken people, driven mad by suffering and wrong, no wonder he warmed in his wooing, and said to himself, while he looked down into the kind, frank, high-bred face, raised up in a trustful glow to meet his, " She is an angel ! Achille, you are very lucky."

On second thoughts, the pair, dallying and pro-longing their intercourse, returned as they came, and crossed the bridge among the willows by the Mousse, where the little church, with its red-tiled square tower and its curé's house, nestled.

There, leaning over the gate of the churchyard, contemplating the graves and crosses,—one of them wreathed with white ribands as well as crowned with immortelles, — stood Monsieur Hubert, the curé, a brown, spare, but powerfully-knit man of sixty, in a narrow collar, large three-cornered hat, and long rusty black coat and sash. Jacqueline immediately crossed over to him, and bent her head, while he raised his hands with a slight gesture of benediction before he greeted her and her kinsman. · The Chevalier returned the greeting gracefully though indifferently.   Babette curtseyed, and then flew off to seize the opportunity of a gossip with a true commère at the village well, their tongues running as fast as the water, and their whole bodies aiding in the endless variety of appropriate gesture.

Monsieur Hubert was not of the most striking type of French priests.   He was neither jovial, like Rohan, the princely cardinal; nor was he unworldly, like Fénélon, the saintly archbishop. But there are many men born soldiers; and such was the curé of Faye, though he was bred a priest. He had a passion for duty and discipline, a genius for command and obedience, while his whole soul loathed dastards and renegades.   He was more feared than loved, though at bottom he was a great Christian, and laboured unremittingly in his calling.   He was well-born, though with a slender patrimony; and in his youth he had won distinction in the Academy, which ought to have recommended him to the quality and the *bels esprits*, when plane geometry and algebra were manias with vain women; but he had never

risen above the humblest rank in the Church.
In his age he had forsaken his charts and pro-
blems, to devote himself to the Georgics and
Bucolics, and the ordinary humanity of his parishioners; a change which should have pleased the
farmers and peasants in his charge. But Monsieur
Hubert had not a wide enough nature, though at
the same time he was, paradoxically, too wide in
his temperament for popularity. He was out of
the common in his very peculiarities; for while
multitudes of Frenchmen were republicans in
theory and absolutists in practice,—writing twenty
volumes of philanthropy, like Mirabeau the elder,
and living the lives of cruel tyrants,—the curé was
an aristocrat in principle and a republican in
deed. He associated with the people, worked for
them, quarrelled with them, dogmatized and
stormed over them, relieved them, and bore
long with them.

Madame at the Tour made a wry face at
Monsieur Hubert; said he was not of her sort;
complained that she could not be converted
under him, but had to rely on private repent-

ance, which was not according to rule. Agathe,
Madame's woman, was still more against the
curé. She threw out dark intimations of Jansen-
ism, and of every saint's turning his or her back
on Faye, since the cure dealt sharply with her at
confession. Neither was the curé of Monsieur's
sort; though Monsieur's misanthropy was much
more tolerant. He only said that the priest cut
him like an east wind. As for the need of energy
in the ecclesiastic, Monsieur could make nothing
of that; there seemed to him no more use for it
than for the east wind. Then the curé was
allowing himself to degenerate; but that was his
affair, not Monsieur's.

It was some compensation to Monsieur Hubert
that those who were fond of him had unquali-
fied faith in him. And among them were Mademoiselle and the Sarts. He, however strict and
wise, had never lost patience with the child
Jacqueline in her catechism; and while he taught
her to respect himself, he had given her a rare
glimpse into the genuine goodness of his heart
by rewarding her with introductions to his pets.

For the curé had pets, and a variety of them,—turtle doves, a Persian cat, an eel in his well,—and was as scrupulous and thoughtful in attending to them as he was assiduous in preaching and teaching, in bleeding and physicking the people. With regard to the last department of his office : he had more than the usual parish priest's or philosophical Monsieur's acquaintance with surgery and medicine ; and he gave advice, drugs, and kitchen stuff to all who needed them, until he pinched himself in his own temperate requirements. Ay, and he looked fierce, and was not grateful, when his parishioners and patients spoke of rewards, or offered him presents at Christmas and Easter. And thus the shallow-minded and purely sensitive among them learned to regard him as the obliged person, and themselves as rather ill-used than otherwise by his cares and sacrifices. In truth, the curé was the veritable aristocrat. He relished conferring favours, but he could not stomach receiving them. And he was forced to take the consequence of what was a proud, ungenial flaw in his gallant character.

Monsieur Hubert had not taken the oaths under
the change of government, and his connection with
his flock was now about to be formally dissolved.
A priest who had sworn to the new constitution was
to supersede him in the small dignities and emolu-
ments of the parish; and he was about to set
out to join a brother in blood and in orders,
whom he had got permission from the bishop
of his diocese to visit at Namur.

Jacqueline thought to take leave of her spi-
ritual father when she crossed the bridge; and it
was by way of dulling the pain of parting that
she recurred to an infinitely sadder, as well as
more irremediable calamity, and said, looking over
into the churchyard at the cross with the white
ribands, "Ah, my father! I see the poor Bénigne's
companions have not yet forgotten her. Dead
at twenty, hélas! what a frightful affliction to her
friends! What are all other misfortunes compared
to this cruel death?"

"Do you think so, Mademoiselle?" asked the
curé, abruptly, facing quite round on Jacqueline
and the Chevalier, and casting a keen glance at

them from under the white eyebrows which contrasted broadly, but not discordantly, with his hale, sunburned face.

"Without doubt," asserted Jacqueline, wondering at his implied objection. "Although I am a Christian and believe in paradise, and although I pray the good God to reconcile me to His will, I think death is terrible to the young and the happy." And Jacqueline, in her own youth and light-heartedness, and the subduing glory of the last few hours, shivered as she looked at the virginal ribands,—the peaceful, cherished, consecrated grave.

"I have seen things more horrible," averred the curé, still looking intently at the two with his brown set face, and speaking with a repressed fervour which he did not always show on the tribune. "Pardon, and listen to a sermon, my Mademoiselle, not in character, and not often preached in the ears of such a young girl as you. My sermon shall consist of warnings. I have known a poor lost creature decoyed and dragged to sin and shame—— The priests employ hard names, Monsieur," he interrupted himself to reply to the undisguised annoyance of Achille de Faye at so unusual a discourse addressed to a young, unmarried, noble woman; "betrayed, I say it, by her adopted mother and her pretended benefactor. You may have heard of her as the beautiful, broken-hearted Circassian, Mademoiselle Aissé. I have seen, again, a gifted, diligent, learned woman, though she was brown and lean as a weasel, mad to be a beauty, and prodigal in Pompons. She could translate the *Principia* of Newton; but she could not conquer her petty ambition, or restrain her frivolous extravagance, or keep the straight line in morals which an ignorant, brutal peasant's wife can preserve. Allons! she was the Venus-Newton of the great Frederic, the Divine Emilia of Arouet Voltaire. I have been received, too, plain as I am now, in the bureau of Madame Dudevant, whose wit was nearest to that of the philosopher of Ferney —the sneering, snarling man whose body was like a lath, his nose and chin shaking hands, and whose head we worship because it is so like an inspired monkey's. If monkeys could reason, their reasoning would be as fine and cutting as his. En revanche, in that bureau (they said the most unique in Paris), where the conversation was perfectly heartless, and the gross corruption universal, the presiding genius of the place—whom her God had afflicted with blindness,—who had been daughter, wife, and mother, exclaimed to another woman, less de-naturalized, 'Ah! you are very happy. I never could love anything.' In fine, I have been at the Court when the Pompadour reigned in the costume of a Diana, or of a nun; when ladies of quality were her waiting-women, and a Knight of St. Louis (pardon, Monsieur!) her steward. And she forced us into a war with Prussia, and cost us millions of treasure and seas of blood, till cruel death, as you call it, came, and her dishonoured corpse was hustled out at a back door of the palace, the King, her master and her lover, looking after her, and, shrug-ging his shoulders, observing to her old parasites, 'The Marquise has rainy weather for her last journey.' Now, are not these things more terrible than death, my child?" he finished, dropping his voice, and passing in a bound from irony to deep, rueful pathos, all the more impressive that it was unexpected, and only to be found in the man on rare occasions.

"Oh! yes," sighed Jacqueline, shocked and grieved; "but why do you tell them to me?"

"Why, indeed, Monsieur the Curé?" remonstrated Achille, warmly. "I grant vice and death are everywhere; but say, then, was it necessary to affront Mademoiselle Jacqueline with these miserable recitals?"

"I have never believed ignorance to be innocence," said the curé, dryly; "nor found the daughters of the noblesse, taken out of their convents, more virtuous women than the daughters of the peasants, brought up with their brothers and their brothers' companions in the fields. It depends on how you treat the truth. You remind me, Monsieur, of an old picture — I think by Orcagna—in the Campo Santo of Pisa. A gay hunting party have come at a turn of the road on the corpses of three princes, when an impatient

man looks aside and holds his nose, while a
patient woman leans her head on her hand and
contemplates the spectacle. The moral is quite
simple. There are some who only distinguish the
stench in vice and death, but there are others
who meet them with a divine pity, an eternal life.
It is because I know Mademoiselle to be good
and true that I have thus spoken," said Monsieur
Hubert, with a gravity which was far removed
from compliment, "and because it may be the
last occasion—you comprehend?—on which I can
address to my pupil a word of counsel before the
snares of the world are around her, and she has
departed beyond my power into quite other hands.
I quit Faye in eight days."

"So soon, my father?" said Jacqueline, hanging
her head, notwithstanding her previous knowledge
of the event, and wondering, with a pang of intuition, whether she would ever again have such
another friend, who would be like a rock on which
she could lean, and who would ask nothing from
her in return but the ennobling remembrance of
her highest interest. Soon Jacqueline forgot all

this, but now she was saying, and meaning it,
"You have been too good to me.   Oh! I will do
all I can to show that I have profited by your
lessons."

Even the Chevalier, who saw clearly that the
curé distrusted him, was at once too magnanimous
and too careless to resent the injury.   What was
it to him that a railing, reforming old priest, the
representative of an institution as near the wall
as his own, undervalued and was disposed to
suspect him?   So he took off his hat and bowed
punctiliously: "I thank you in the name of
Mademoiselle my cousin for your sermon.   Permit
me, on my own account, to assure you"—and the
young man looked with a triumphant, fearless,
not unfriendly expression at the priest, before
he looked lovingly at Jacqueline, — "Permit
me to assure you that I am sorry that your absence will prevent me from engaging your
services in a personal matter,—a matter entirely
between ourselves, you comprehend, Monsieur the
Curé,—yet not at all without the consent of Monsieur and Madame."

"Thank you, Monsieur. Ah! Well, I could not have done it without both pleasure and pain," said Monsieur Hubert, plainly, accepting the propitiation with a *sang froid* and a reserve all his own.

Monsieur Hubert continued leaning over the churchyard gate, and looking after the lovers till they were halfway up the village street. "He is not very bad, that boy, for a noble," he mused; "and they will be purified should they ever come out of the furnace. After all, they have some faith, while the middle class is fast losing itself in the sans-culottes, and sinking to their level, —adopting domestic virtue of an unconsciously Christianized pagan kind, together with the cold reasoning of deism, the selfish calculation of money-making, and the outrageous excesses of a rank, wild libertinism and atheism. There is no soundness and no germ of a higher growth to save them. Though he is not very bad for his lot, that young chevalier, I fear for my girl Jacqueline. I could have more rest in my mind for her—my best friend, after Michel Sart, old fool that I am—if she lay here beside the poor consumptive Bénigne, than going there, healthy and radiant, thrilling in every nerve, with the handsome aristocrat, who may weary of her and be false to her in a month, if La Force and the Luxembourg spare him so long, and he be not guillotined and she be not an inconsolable widow within the time."

"Man proposes, but God disposes." Within a few days the Chevalier left the Tour, not alone, but accompanied by no less a person than Monsieur. He was going on business to the next province, with the intention of returning to Faye along with its master, to proceed briskly in the preparations for his establishment in his future home. But instead of this, Monsieur returned without the Chevalier, very cynical and very gentle, as he was wont to be when things went particularly wrong with him. Then followed, not the Chevalier, but a note from the Chevalier to Jacqueline. She was much fluttered by a liberty and an advance to intimacy so uncommon. The note was short and constrained, and more flighty than expressive of ardent affection and devotion ; but the circumstances which called it forth excused the indiscretion even to Madame.

" My much-honoured and well-beloved cousin," it ran, " I am forced to write to you to beg you to let me know whether Monsieur your father has returned in safety. I fear to address himself, lest the letter should miscarry in his absence ; and to write to Madame might attract more attention than to write thus to you. I have bad news, my beautiful. The entire proscription of the priests, and the ruin of *him* who has been resisting it, is too sure. Our rents are gone to the last farthing. The powers won't even leave the *quasi* nobles their pigeon-houses to take refuge in. Oh, Jacqueline, if you hear tidings you did not expect, remember I can no longer help myself, while I remain always, your faithful friend, ACHILLE RENE DE FAYE."

After the excitement and glory of receiving the letter—during which its contents were of no consequence, — Jacqueline was a little puzzled and pained by these lines. Nevertheless it was her first letter from Achille, and she thought it a very

interesting letter, in its half mournfulness, half
recklessness ; and was very much obliged to her
parents for their permission to answer it.

Jacqueline was in her own room in Madamé's
tourelle — a novice's room, fresh and simple, all
draped with spotless white dimity. Her presence
was further indicated by her birds, her little lion
dog Nerina on its cushion, and her books: a
translation of *Clarissa Harlowe*, and still more
doubtful works, such as the *Nouvelle Héloise*
of Jean Jacques, close to the *Imitation* of
Thomas à Kempis—books, indeed, which cannot
be mentioned without an explanation that their
presence was another testimony that "to the pure
all things are pure," and that such proximities
existed unchallenged and uncondemned in the
most virtuous houses, and under the eyes of the
most innocent girls of France. Standards as well
as generations change. When Marie Antoinette
had to make application to the Convention for a
book to instruct and amuse her little son, her
selection was *Gil Blas*.

There was Jacqueline, seated at her pupitre.

prepared to answer her letter,—her lace sleeves tucked up from her fair arms, her light brown curls shed back from her open forehead. Madame de Sevigné might write quires of paper from Brittany to her daughter in Provence every week of the year; and of course writing was to her but another and only less delightful mode of speaking. But ladies who had much ado to live, to whom mere life became a stirring excitement, grew chary of their letters in Jacqueline's day. And this was Jacqueline's first love-letter.

Strange to tell, the words were slow of coming, and Jacqueline tapped her white forehead with her pen very importunately, and sat with her curved red lips apart for a long time without result. If girls will fall in love with their own fancies in the shape of handsome gallant young men, with whom they have nothing else in common but youth and station,—with whom they can have nothing like communion, and of whose sneers, when they are not with them and dazzled by their fascination, they have a very lively apprehension ;—then, of course, letter-writing, even to the clearest-minded and the most single-hearted, will be a perplexing, laborious task.

"My much-honoured cousin," Jacqueline began, in the same high and kingly strain as Achille, but thinking it more maidenly to leave out the other clause of "well-beloved," even to her promised husband. "I am very glad to inform you that Monsieur arrived at home three days ago, in good health, and not too much fatigued by his little journey. I am very sorry for your bad news, Monsieur." Pausing, at a loss what next to say, Jacqueline raised her head, and saw reflected in the diamond-shaped mirror opposite her, the broad, warm, shrewd face of Babette, her solid throat elongated and stuck out like the neck of a goose; her wide, expressive mouth screwed into the small dimensions of a button-hole. Babette had learned to read and write along with Mademoiselle at the Tour; and here she was, making use of a part of her accomplishments, without her mistress's leave, over her mistress's shoulder. The result may be guessed.

Jacqueline was indignant; but the group was

comical, and there was no harm done. On the
contrary, the interruption freed Jacqueline from
the horns of a dilemma. She did not turn round,
but wrote in a legible hand, "I would say more,
but my maid Babette is standing behind my chair,
reading what I write." A loud thump was heard
almost simultaneously with the penning of the
sentence. It was Babette leaping back as far as
the wall of the room would let her; the same
moment she cried, in a tone of insulted innocence,
" Me, Mademoiselle! I assure you I have not read
a word!"

"Oh, Babette, how droll you are!" protested
Jacqueline, holding her slight sides, and shaking
with a peal of girlish laughter. " You will make me
split with laughing. If you had not read the accusation, how could you have known that I blamed
you? Oh, you are caught, caught, my good
Babette!"

"Yes — there, Mademoiselle!" Babette threw
down her cards instantly, turning from a rose to a
peony, but submitting to fate, and not losing sight
of her philosophy. " How can a poor girl like

me practise the reading and writing your family
were so good as to give me unless in stolen mouth-
fuls? and how am I to gain knowledge otherwise
I should like to know? But I would never betray
you, my little Mademoiselle," concluded Babette,
at once altering her tone, and speaking with an
imploring vehemence quite different from the beginning of her confession. "Never, never!" And
great Babette set herself to sob and cry like a con-
victed, but falsely judged baby.

"My life! No, my girl. Why do you make so
much work about it? You are not a Judas."
Jacqueline hastened to pet and comfort the girl
her senior, patting her on the shoulder, and caressing her. "It is not for me to listen at doors
or read letters over people's shoulders. I was not
brought up to that; but I suppose it runs in the
blood of femmes-de-chambre. Though, if I were
you, Babette, I would be more than a femme-
de-chambre : I would be a true and noble woman,
like La Sarte, on whom everybody can rely. As
for betrayal, I would as soon suspect myself of
treachery," and Jacqueline threw her arms again

round the neck of her old playfellow and lifelong companion, who hung her head, wiped her black eyes with her bright-coloured apron, and writhed in the kind grasp. "I had no more to say to the Chevalier, Ba-ba, that is the truth; and this end, which is also the truth, is as good as another, and saves the anguish of composition. You, Barbe, wait till I sign my name, and see my letter an accomplished fact."

"If I were you, I would put something more tender, Mademoiselle," suggested Babette, with a little diffidence because of her late transgression. "Suppose the poor Chevalier is to wear it in his bosom till you see him again, and waste it away with a hundred thousand kisses. Sainte Geneviéve! I would give him something better worth wearing and kissing."

"Fy, fy! to bid me write words of love to a man who is not yet my husband. I wonder what Madame would say? Wait till we are married, and then we shall see—we shall see how I will love the poor, brave boy. He is so brave and so handsome and distinguished, Babette, like—I do not know what," broke off Jacqueline in simple ecstasy.

"I know, Mademoiselle," chimed in Babette eagerly, with a smack of her lips; "he tastes like well-sugared galette and sparkling gooseberry water. Is it not so?"—sending Jacqueline into another fit of giddy laughter.

Very soon she was to laugh no more; and already she was calmed down by one of those intuitions which come most frequently to children and childlike men and women. For speaking pensively, almost mournfully, she said: "As to wearing and kissing my letter, my dear, that is no longer the mode; and Monsieur Achille is very much à la mode. He loves me in his own way when he is by me, I believe; and you see by this letter he remembers me a little when he is away from me. But what would you? He is a man of the world, and a nobleman; and though his beard is not full grown yet, he is so much wiser, more clever, grander than I. Do you think I did not notice that? Still I shall be Dame de Faye," put in the girl, drawing herself up with pretty, assumed, hereditary dignity. "However, he is a chevalier so proud that I predict it will rather be me who will wear and kiss his letters. And what will you again, my Babette?" she finished, with a revulsion of feeling, throwing off her pretty air of stateliness, and looking beautiful and womanly in a faint glimmer and glory of self-sacrifice. "Should not the woman love the most, since we are not on a desert island to be everything to each other?"

"I do not see that the woman should love the most," argued Babette, doggedly; "but she does it, fault of me!" she admitted, impetuously. "I am bound to confess it. I think it must be as a punishment for her sins, because she gave Monsieur Adam that miserable apple in the garden, which sticks in the man's throat to this day."

Does the woman love the most? My friend Babette, you may live to find out in your own experience.

CHAPTER IV.

THE LAST OF THE EMIGRANTS, PETRONILLE DE CROÏ— BABETTE'S USELESS PILGRIMAGE.

LIFE went fast in France during the Revolution years. The whole course was got over in a few months or even days, without the slackening of bridle or girth. "We live ten years in twenty-four hours," said Manon Phlippon, after she was the wife of the Spartan Frenchman, Roland de la Plaitière ; and the poor Filla Dolorosa—the prison flower—passed from youth to age in that brief space which cost her her father, mother, aunt, and little brother.

Monsieur the Curé had celebrated his last mass, taken leave of his sheep, and was gone. When he stood and faced the flock as their shepherd for the last time, he told them in his sonorous tones, which inspired strong confidence, because they never faltered, " My children, you and I are joined in wedlock before the Lord, in a union which cannot be broken. I am yours and you are mine. I do not know if I will see you again ; but if the Lord send better days, and if He give me life, I will come back to you." And the listeners—not only those who loved the valiant brown face, but many who shrank from it, some even who hated it, were assured that the man who had fought against their sins and stupidity these thirty years, would keep his word.

The *Ça ira* and the *Marseillaise* had come to be sung in din and discordance within the royal chapel of the Tuileries. " He hath put down the mighty, and exalted them of low degree," was the text thundered into the quaking ears of princely worshippers. Another insurrection—that of the 9th and 10th August—had broken out at Paris, when the Swiss mountaineers died in vain for French royalty. Louis and his family took refuge in the National Assembly, and sat fourteen hours in the reporters' box listening to the suspension of the royal authority, and the practical deposition of the king. Yet he was able to eat the wing of a chicken and drink a glass of wine, just as he had called for bread and cheese when stopped at Varennes; while Marie Antoinette, her blue eyes tearless, but her Saxon hair blanched white, flushed darkly at his supineness, and needed no refreshment to help her to clasp her sleeping children to her knees. She showed herself to be, as she was termed, " the best man among them." The next movement of the poor helpless martyr family—one of countless martyr families, and only conspicuous in its reverses and its misery—was to the Temple.

In the meantime the announcement that Paris was given up to blood and fire, and the country in hourly danger of invasion, travelled fast to the provinces, calling forth rushes to town-halls, harangues of heated citizens, the assembling of the National Guard, the waving of flags, and the stirring up of passions already brutal in their fury. France was girdled by enemies — Prussians, Austrians, Spaniards, Sardinians. At

Paris the church bells were torn down, and the very leaden coffins of the dead dug up, to be melted and cast afresh into munitions of war. Leather-skinned bands of Marseillais, like raging beasts of prey, came to Paris on the invitation of Barbaroux, still better to teach the Parisians their hymn. Ishmaelites of a vitiated civilization, whose hand was against every man and every man's hand against them, who were aliens to the mass of the population,—branded men of the hulks and the galleys, utterly debased and ferocious, drawn by the scent of carrion and plunder, —were streaming singly or in tens and scores along the roads to Paris.

It was the lull before the wild roar of the tempest, but had every symptom of a tremendous battle of the elements. And an awe fell beforehand upon the quiet, passive inhabitants of the country. The remnants of the old dominant class, lingering and lurking in their retreats, were looked upon, in the sultry, stormy August weather, as hordes of secret plotters, among the full grapes, waiting for the vintage and the slaughter.

The very air must have been oppressive, and
laden with portents; for even children and dumb
animals—girls like Jacqueline, who laughed no
longer, and her silky poodle Nerina, which whined
and begged because its mistress had ceased to
play with it—panted and cowered under the fatal
influence.

Jacqueline danced no more gavottes or entre-
chats as she escaped from the evening card
party. For card-playing, like eating and drinking, continued; the seniors, however chilled and
heavy at heart, being consummate masters and
mistresses of their outward behaviour. And the
girl had no heart to act differently from her elders,
her youthful laughter having died away in a qualm
of fright and dismay. She boasted no more of
being Citoyenne Jacqueline, which was destined
to be her distinctive name. She began to wonder
piteously whether it was worse to eat bread made
of heather and die of hunger, like the wretched
peasant from whose deal coffin Louis the Well-
beloved backed impulsively, as he hunted in
the forest; or to weep day and night in the

Temple ; or to have relations dragged from her
and shut up in some of the numerous gorged prisons,
never to be heard of again in this world, though
their blood should cry day and night for vengeance
to the Lord of all worlds ; or to be herself caught,
shamefully entreated, and murdered. She had
sinned against God ; but what ill had she done to
the world ? Her heavenly Father had pardoned
her—would not her human brother, too, pardon her
supposed offence, whatever it might be, and spare
the young life, the taking of which could be of
no avail to the thirsty soil of France, parched
and gaping as it was for blood ?

But if the worst came to the worst, could not
Jacqueline make her death of some avail ? Might
she not be strengthened to offer the sacrifice which
was so small, but which would be accepted because
it was her all ? Yes, Jacqueline moped and
dreamt. She was haunted with that feverish,
morbid ghost of heroism which drove on the
young girls of France, and wooed them with the
ghastly glamour of horror to ponder over the story
of Jephthah's daughter among the mountains of

Israel, and of Judith in the Syrian camp. The times were so unnatural and exceptional, that they pointed to an unnatural and exceptional deliverance. French girls have a predisposition to such half-sublime, spectral delusions, derived from the story of the Maid of Orleans, whom Frenchmen of the Greek and classic era scoffed at, but which Frenchwomen devoutly believed. Already Charlotte Corday, with Corneille's blood in her blue veins, and his moon-struck, one-sided noble rant on her passionate scarlet lips, read of the Hebrew women, on her simple white bed, or in her country walks, where the breeze blew over the fruit-laden orchards, and over the briny waves that wash green Normandy. Woe to her! for that was long after she had ceased to read of the Canaanitish woman, out of whose daughter the Son of Mary—the good Master, the God of Life—cast the devil, whose serpent tongue might have one day hissed into her ear that she was exalted above all law, human and divine—that crime was virtue and death life.

Jacqueline was delivered from this strange dan-

ger by the armour of faith, which continued to
gird her tender spirit. Reason was too thread-
bare, cold, and loveless a garment for her warm,
reverent affections. Her God was somewhere in
yon blue sky; He cared for her, had suffered
for her, though He mysteriously permitted these
sufferings around her; and the words He had
left her were, "Vengeance is mine, saith the
Lord;" "Love thine enemy; do good to them
which hate you, and pray for them which despite-
fully use you and persecute you."

And she was but a girl, whose mind was
diverted from the delirium of these visions by a
private grief, in the midst of the general affliction. She had neither seen nor heard of Achille
de Faye since his visit and his letter; and in
this interval her marriage with him for the present had become purely impossible. Would the
Chevalier's life be darkened if she were killed by
accident in such a massacre as had occurred in
some of the unhappy districts? Or if she did
some dreadful act, and were killed by design,
would he mourn a little for her? Or, worse

still—and the thought wrung tears from her—had Achille forgotten her so speedily? Would he seek her no more? Had he cast her aside in their common misfortunes as an incumbrance and an affliction? She was so young and so humble, even in her spurts of haughtiness and wilfulness, and in her French girlishness, that she had not woke up to the woman's pride which would yet blaze out and scorch up all such tears.

In this convulsed state of existence, it was a relief to the inhabitants of the Tour de Faye to receive a letter from a family of old friends and equals, announcing a visit, and soliciting a few days' lodging. The friends were Monsieur and Madame de Lussac, and their widowed daughter, Madame de Croï.

This family had been so fortunate as to procure, through powerful influence, one of the latest passports for emigration, and were now on their way to the nearest coast town. It was not safe or friendly for them to lodge in an inn. The occasion was ominous; but the tidings sounded like a return to the old order and the old courtesies of life.

In the thought of receiving visitors and entertaining guests, the family of Faye were tempted to forget the times, to forget that they themselves were in threatened straits for provisions to supply their own daily table, and would be in actual want were it not that Maitre Michel the registrar, and his greater brother Citizen Jonquille, the deputy up in Paris, were honest and true, and prevented the impending confiscation of the whole Faye domain,—refraining from serving themselves as heirs to their old feudal lord, like other registrars and deputies. And in the thought the poor aristocrats of the Tour, living from hand to mouth, on the favour of their servants, accomplished a more splendid feat: they nearly succeeded in blotting out of their minds that their necks too were confiscated to that colossal, deformed idol the Nation, growing in its huge, misshapen bulk while men slept. In truth, if the unhappy nobility of France had not had the faculty of throwing off their loads, and disporting themselves now and then, they would have been crushed betimes, and would not have required to be guillotined, drowned, or shot.

When Jacqueline learned, by the credentials of a courier in advance of the glass-and-leather berline, that the Chevalier—her kinsman, lover, bridegroom—was actually in the train of the Lussacs, travelling to greet her again, she was excited beyond measure, was inconsiderately gay, and unscrupulously blest. What were the privations and risks of next month, next week, to a girl of sixteen, who had the restoration of her lover, cheerful company, grand society, and three clear days before her?

What a running up and down in the old Tour de Faye, on the part of its sadly abridged staff of domestics and their leaders! How old Paul's stiff joints creaked; and how Agathe, with her red hair and ferret eyes, groaned ostentatious Aves; and how Babette screamed and scolded, and bore out the carping assertion, " Women scream before the culprit appears, and for a century after he

has vanished!" And so with the satellites in the
lower regions—the cook and the porteress.

How witty, and not at all incommoded, Madame
was, in her distant audience chamber. How
amused Monsieur was in his philosophical way,
until the fracas became so deafening that he
had to betake himself to his tourelle, and leave
the combatants to conduct the engagement without restraint from his presence. How Jacqueline
ran about with the selfish, fond, foolish song
ringing in her ears, " He is coming again. What
does it signify though Prague was taken once?
It is he. He will be here. I shall see him.
What will Madame de Croï be like? She is
beautiful and admired. Does he admire her?
What shall I wear to be amiable in his eyes?"
Oh! how much better it is to look down the dusty
chaussée, among the walnut trees, for the great
chariot, than to watch Sylvain the butcher hailing
the horrible ragged wayfarers, questioning them in
their rough patois, treating them to a glass of
cider, talking and laughing with them in loud
speech and laughter.

About an hour past noon, to the "crack! crack!" of postillions, the ringing of bells on the horses' trappings, the rattling of wheels, the barking of imprisoned dogs, and all the old pomp and circumstance—the berline clattered and tumbled, under its mountain of luggage, into the gate of the conciergerie, and then up to the Tour.

Out of the berline leaped lightly the elegant Chevalier. Then a little old man, with powdered toupée, little three-cornered hat, silk stockings, and old velvet coat complete, stepped slowly down. Behold Monsieur the Marquis de Lussac, of right noble lineage, and once owner of a princely extent of territory. He is luckier than most émigrés, and has part of his large fortune securely invested in foreign funds, sufficient to maintain his family in affluence, and to afford a fresh dot to Madame de Croï, his daughter,—a childless widow, the hoards of whose late husband were swallowed up in the insatiable coffers of the Nation. Monsieur the Marquis felt carefully and apprehensively, with his five long delicate-looking

talons, surrounded by fluttering cob-web cuffs, in
the cavernous depths of the caravan. What was
he poking his velvet and laced arms about for?
For Madame the Marquise de Lussac? No. For
Madame de Croï? Still less. For Sylphide and
Fidéle, the barking dogs? Not at all. Neither
was it for his family papers, his armorial plate, nor
the picture of the Pierced Heart which hung in
his father's oratory. It was for none of these,
though he loved them all, and would have shed
his few drops of dried up blood for them, as
gallantly as his ancestors shed theirs under Turenne
and the Marshal Luxemburg. Monsieur dug out
his treasure safe, and looked up enraptured. It
was his silver cooking apparatus—his saucepans,
basting spoons, and cullenders; his little chest
of sauces, spices, and dried herbs. Without these
he never journeyed a step, and with them he
could rival the masterpieces of the most gifted
and perfectly trained of cooks. Some of the
grand old quality were philosophers, architects,
astronomers, writers of pasquilles or madrigals,
doctors, fiddlers, and cooks—all combined. Mon-

sieur de Lussac was more modest and wise. He contented himself with being one thing superlatively. He was, before even his old master, the prince of cooks.

The Chevalier handed out Madame de Lussac and Madame de Croï. Each was impeded by a struggling, yelping lapdog, fastened with a silk riband to her girdle; and each bore on her mind a weight of bandboxes of the first importance, and was accompanied by a demoiselle de compagnie, gabbling in her turn, listening to her special shrill instructions, cracked or otherwise.

This was no time for greetings and introductions. Madame de Faye was far too well informed, and had too much respect for her own claims, to think of such a thing for a moment. "Let the ladies be shown to their chambers. We will meet at supper." After this dictum, Madame comfortably, and with piquant amusement, inspected the arrival undisguisedly from her window.

Jacqueline was inexperienced. She wanted to do something,—to go up with shy but open arms to everybody. She rashly ventured down to her

father, standing uncovered in the great doorway,
beneath the stone carving of the three falcons
and the two savages, prepared to receive, embrace, and bow over the hands of his guests,
and to assure them of his thousand welcomes.
She hovered behind Monsieur de Faye, and saw
the empressement of the principal actors in the
scene ; and, in the distance, the villagers of Faye,
the children, and the goats, on the qui vive
for what had waxed into a rare event in their
annals.

Madame de Croï spared a moment to notice
Jacqueline: "Is this your young cousin?" she
asked of the Chevalier, who had hardly snatched
an opportunity to kiss his little mistress's hand.
"My young friend, I shall be enchanted to make
your acquaintance," pronounced Madame de Croï,
graciously, as she at last passed across the terrace
on the arm of Achille.

Very innocent, kind words apparently ; but
they jarred on Jacqueline's quick ear, and did not
please her. Why should she be addressed as a
young friend by a woman not above two years

her senior? Why should Madame de Croï speak
of *her* making the acquaintance which ought,
by right, to be a transaction between the two—
unless the fact of her having been married con-
ferred an advantage on her side, which she did not
hesitate to claim? Madame de Croï was in this
position; and it was because Jacqueline had come
on the carpet in transition times, and was tinged
with republicanism, that she did not yield gracefully and like a rational creature. Jacqueline did
not understand it. She only knew that she did
not like Madame de Croï's looking at her and
speaking of her in a sweet way, as from high to
low. And she did not believe Achille liked it
either, because, marvellous to relate, though he
was the Chevalier, "genteel, always genteel," he
was flurried as he spoke to her and inquired for
Madame the Baronne her mother.

Jacqueline was not wiser than the rest of the
world who walk in darkness. She did not guess,
when she came down imprudently and ingenu-
ously into the stir of the alighting on the terrace that August day, that she was hurrying to

meet her fate; she did not recognise that the
young lady in the travelling roquelaire and the
gipsy hat was her mortal enemy; nor feel her
skin rise like the skin of a turkey; nor mutter
gibberish about stars and destiny, picked up
from Mesmer and Cagliostro, as did Achille de
Faye when he encountered Sylvain the butcher.
She did nothing except conceive an instantaneous,
violent prejudice against the person who had
spoiled her meeting with her kinsman.

Madame de Lussac had not leisure even to look
at Jacqueline; she was so engrossed with her dog,
her caged birds, and her aggravated and aggra-
vating demoiselle de compagnie.

Jacqueline accorded her decided preference to
Monsieur the Marquis, who was triumphant in
having made an accurate inventory of his saucepans, and in his quick apprehension of her
identity. " Mademoiselle your daughter, De
Faye? Ah! I knew such a narcisse could only
be the child of you and Madame. Mon enfant,
will you permit an old man whom your freshness
makes young again to pay you his devoirs?"

Jacqueline was glad when the party retired for rest and refreshment to what was the œil-de-bœuf of Faye,—feeling, half-sorrowfully, half-pettishly, that the eagerly expected event had grievously disappointed her; and that the reception of the distinguished strangers had fallen flat with the first flourish of trumpets.

In consideration of the requirements of the travellers, who had dined on the road, Madame the Chatelaine de Faye received at four o'clock that day; and the supper, as Monsieur de Lussac ascertained delicately, but without question, was arranged for seven o'clock. By five the circle in Madame's luxurious room was complete — that punctilious, refined French circle, in which there could be no tête-à-tête ;—where a leader (generally a woman), or a succession of leaders, conducted the conversation, and the men stood deferentially behind the high-backed chairs, as at an opera, treating skilfully the topics the women touched lightly ; and where each introduced his or her witticism in turn, as opportunity offered, so that there was no monopoly, and the ball of conversation was kept up with exceeding dexterity and grace. A circle arbitrary and artificial; apt to be affected and insipid; and sometimes desperately roué and wicked under the surface. But the conversation was wonderfully polished, and on occasions, dazzlingly brilliant, although not without an unacknowledged shade of mystery and expectation, which, like the Rembrandt duskiness, was replete with romance.

See there Madame the Baronne—a picture in herself, and thoroughly herself, neither more nor less. The robed, rouged, plumed woman, with the singularly mobile, high, aristocratic features, and the graceful arms and hands, told her anecdotes, announced her whims, betrayed her foibles, —and manifested a combination of art and nature so rare and complete, that no mortal could tell where the one began and the other ended.

The Marquise was not equal to her friend; she was a washed-out, streaky copy of her. She fondly embraced her dearest, best Madame de Faye, like one school-girl encountering another at the end of a week's parting; and she inquired with the

utmost warmth for the black and white curly
darling Nerina, requiring a funeral oration on
the darling's departed mother Tristaine.   She
expressed a little detached, spasmodic interest in
common friends, muttering a blank "Ciel!" or
two over this Comte and that Prince, and the
miserable wreck of the country from which she
and her family were escaping for their lives.   In
both instances she huddled her sentences together
in evident panic, to which she dared not give
breath or speech, but was forced to bury it in
her own bosom, where the poor woman had a
chance of dying of it.   And then she languished
on her fauteuil in a state of exhaustion.   Madame de Faye, at the climax of their friendship, said of Madame de Lussac, with sovereign
contempt, that the Marquise had only possessed
the weakest crumb of ideas at the best, and since
she fell into agonies of poltroonery, the crumb
had been privately soaked in a wretched pickle
of tears, so that there was but a half-dissolved
morsel of her left.

Monsieur de Lussac existed principally in con-

nection with meals; but there could not be a
huger mistake than to suppose him, in consequence, a nobody. On the contrary, wherever
he went he became the presiding genius of
the kitchen, where, asking and receiving carte
blanche, he installed himself in the admiring confidence of the chief of the department. He entered so completely, heart and soul, into business—
threw himself so disinterestedly and generously
into the choicest, most recherché achievements
for the entertainment of the château or hôtel in
which he was guest, that, like his less endowed
Marquise, he emerged from his field of enter-
prise in a collapsed condition, sat with half-
closed eyes or slumbered outright till the moment
of trial, when the fillet à la Du Barry or the
salade à la volaille rewarded his great qualifica-
tions, and covered him with glory. Then the
Marquis was at his culminating point, — then
he not only carved and sent round a dish as a
finished artiste would dispense it, but he rendered it historical, æsthetical, poetical, religious:
"Does the dish please you, Madame? I am

ravished to hear it—a bagatelle, quite simple. The
kernel of the affair had its birth at a Lent supper of
the great Cardinal's. But let us await the soufflet,
—also a virginal dish, with a still more splendid
origin. This soufflet aux dattes was brought from
Egypt by no meaner personages than Saint Louis
and Marguerite of Provence."

A spectator, above all a convive, could easily
discover that the withered, bright-eyed old nobleman had lived at a time when dainty eating
and famine were two of the· institutions of
France ; and when supper was one of the things
to live for. He was not malicious or tyrannical ;
rather, like most unrivalled men of science, he
was good-natured and affable. That he was like-
wise perfectly careless of all outside his own range
was an unlucky, not a remarkable abuse of his
powers. Monsieur de Lussac would really have
preferred the whole universe to profit by his côte-
lettes and crêmes. Since that was impossible,
he believed sincerely that men might as well perish
of inanition, as swallow garlic soup with a taste of
artichokes.

At the present hour Monsieur the Marquis, though receiving a temporary stimulus from the prospect of assisting at the supper at the Tour, was sunk in courteous but all-pervading sadness: " I have never seen a finer year for truffles. Mushrooms will be magnificent. Yet I go away, I quit France. And they tell me, in savage England mushrooms are either served with their rude bifteck or treated as poison. What a country! What morals! What manners! With us the Gauls knew better."

The responsibility and the credit of sustaining the conversation in a manner becoming the country and the age, fell, after Madamé de Faye, on Madame de Croï. . The Chevalier was certainly out of sorts, and only by fits and starts did he do himself justice. He wore the white uniform of his regiment, which, in the persons of the private soldiers, had gone over to the Republic, or, in the persons of the officers, was advancing under the Austrian and Prussian standards to the heights of Argonne. Perhaps the uniform suggested chequered thoughts of the past. Perhaps it was the tight white coat which lent to his handsome face and figure a furtive sallowness and leanness.

But Petronille de Croï atoned for all deficiencies; she was, beyond comparison, the most striking person present, after Madame de Faye. She was a handsome, beautiful, witty young woman of the world, in whom only the finest judgement could detect flaw or failure. She was not overwhelmed by adversity. She had more than mere education—she had that inheritance of spontaneous equanimity which belongs both to vigorous and to nicely balanced minds.

Beside Petronille, Jacqueline was but a charming child. There is a vast amount of outward difference, easy of comprehension in France, between the young unmarried girl and the woman, equally young, who has been at the head of an establishment, and is mistress of herself and her actions. Jacqueline, in her white gown tucked up out of everybody's way, her little blue neckerchief à la Marie Antoinette, and her brown hair in negligence on her shoulders, appeared more youthful than she really was. Madame de Croï, at eighteen, affected, justifiably as custom went, quite a different style of dress, one much nearer that of the Baronne and the Marquise, but still in keeping with her years, and calculated to enhance her remarkable order of beauty.

Fashions had not yet taken the bound to short waists, Arab turbans, and the scant drapery of the Greek statues. The oriental and the classic devotions are to be attributed to the Directory and the first years of the Consulship, when even sane directors received "le petit caporal" with the "redingot gris," in the extraordinary costume, for Frenchmen, of bare legs and Roman togas. About the same time—oh! poor volatile nation, heroically theatrical the one day, meretriciously stage-struck the next,—Frenchwomen glided and attitudinized in the shawl dance, under what was no better than the houri guidance of Emma Lady Hamilton.

Fashion was still stately and decorous, although pompous; and Madame de Croï gave in -her adherence to the old mode, which modern authorities have declared remains unsurpassed in splendour and dignity. It consisted, in her case, of a complete suit of lilac brocade frosted with silver, and included hair-powder, which bestowed on the hair a tint "subdued and ashy." With regard to which a competent writer assures us eloquently: "This manner of moderating the harshness of the tone of the hair lent to the face much softness and to the eyes extraordinary splendour. The forehead, entirely uncovered, lost itself in the pale shades of the hair, and appeared broader and purer. Every woman had a noble air." This appearance of nobleness—a broad, regal fore-head, and flashing, melting eyes—constituted the distinctive beauty of Madame de Croï; and, to crown it, in place of Jacqueline's daisy freshness of complexion, she had a creamy, satin skin— to which she did not contribute a grain of rouge or a fly of a patch, and which looked too deli-cate for the rough wind to blow upon. Very refined and peerlessly noble looked the face of Petronille de Croï; and not supine or apathetic, but lit up with the charm of her spirituelle conversation.

The talk was of books, the French comedy,

the old Court; with details from the capital.
There was a little said of political giants and
demagogues, but less of that than of anything
else—the subject being slippery and uncertain,
with unhappy tendencies.   In all its branches
Madame de Croï proved herself mistress of the
tree of knowledge.   She had read the philosophers, or abridgments of them, from D'Alembert
and Diderot to Voltaire and Saint Simon, and had
her superficial but crystal-clear echo of their con-
clusions.   She had listened to the reasoning of the
ecclesiastics.   She had seen the pasteboard kings
and queens as well as the real ones; and could
criticise keenly the meaning of a gesture or the
effect of a tone.   She had known eyewitnesses
to the story of the Diamond Necklace—"every
tassel a man's fortune."

" Of course the Queen was innocent," pronounced
Petronille, in her light sarcastic manner; "and
Rohan was imprisoned, and La Motte scourgéd.
But—what will you?—it was all the same to the
Queen's reputation—there was so much likelihood
in the tale."

Alas! poor, susceptible, lavish Marie Antoinette
—it was such light verdicts, exaggerated and darkened elsewhere with a malignant foulness that had
no limits, which stained past redemption her royal
fame—peradventure honest as any peasant's.

Petronille had received La Fayette when the
blue colour of the National Guard filled Paris
streets like one sea. "But then there were the
red facings," she said, "which frightened away all
the fishes. I believe Blondinet, as they called
the gallant general, before jests were exploded at
the Tuileries, mounted the ultramarine because
of his complexion."

She had been present at the Feast of Pikes, the
"I swear it!" in the Champ de Mars, and had
assisted in the proceedings which went on busily
for weeks, when barrows of earth were incessantly
wheeled to and from the Altar of the Country
and the Amphitheatre of the People, by states-
men, soldiers, priests, young girls of rank in zephyr
muslin and tricolour scarfs, amidst the "Vivats!"
of the delirious multitude. "A demoiselle trips
against a mound," recounted Petronille; "at the

instant an avocat starts forward to raise her; but no, she draws back disdainfully. Her father makes her a rapid sign, she extends her hand with grace to a workman in a filthy carmagnole; 'You are my true brother to-day,' she says, divinely. My friends, what applause!"

After long seclusion in privation and danger, it was a treat to the Faye set to listen to so accomplished a speaker. But in conversational power there was as great a difference between Jacqueline de Faye's and Petronille de Croï's minds as that between their bodies. Jacqueline's intuitions were from the heart; Petronille's from the head. Jacqueline's heart bled for the woes of both King and beggar; and when she laughed, it was with them, not at them,—a sister's laugh. Petronille's head noted all mortal errors and inconsistencies, and mocked at their coarseness, their smallness, with an intense, unsparing, unrelenting ridicule. Thus nothing could surpass the few bold, subtle touches,—always within the conventional bounds of her sex and rank,—by which Petronille could convey unfortunate Monsieur Capet's stolidity, upright Bailly's vacillation, this worthy bourgeoise's low ambition, and that pious ex-nun's prudish coquetry. Indeed, as the world goes, Petronille's talent was formed for appreciation.

Such were the individual characters and opinions, not conspicuously, but covertly met and opposed to each other in Madame de Faye's apartment. And just as talent is confident and dominating, and genius shrinking and self-depreciatory, so Jacqueline de Faye, on her trial in her mother's room this August evening, collapsed into seeming insignificance before Petronille de Croï. And yet she was the same Jacqueline who had been so splendid, yon June day, in the hamlet and the ravine. It was her turn then ; it was the tide at the full in her affairs. Now the tide was on the ebb, and ebbing fast ; while Petronille flashed and sparkled, and perfumed the little society with her penetration, her tact, her varied graphicness, for ever running into irony. Jacqueline might be a narcisse as Monsieur the Marquis had said. But it was a poor, tiny, spring narcisse, drooping and dwindling on its stalk, in the heat ; while

Petronille was the summer rose, whose erect cup was constantly expanding, showing daintier tints, and diffusing sweeter odours. The more Petronille shone and sang (figuratively), the more Jacqueline put her finger in her mouth and hung her head on one side (figuratively).

It was not black envy which was chilling and blighting Jacqueline; it was not the thought, "How poor a creature I am in comparison with Petronille de Croï! How much I would give to look, to speak like her! How Monsieur and Madame, my parents, would be proud of me, how Achille would adore me, then!" Perhaps she did feel all this, although she had an innate conviction, in the depth of her soul, that she was superior to Petronille, even that the sounding-line of her sympathy went fathoms deeper into human nature than the steel needle of Petronille's sarcasm, and that her gauge brought up gold while Petronille's found nothing anywhere save dross.

It was the Gothic fever fit of jealousy that was scorching Jacqueline's proud, sensitive heart, tormenting and sickening it, shrivelling it before its time, humbling it in the dust. And that large young heart was still fast bound in the swaddling-clothes of French girlhood, and could not rise and assert the dignity of its womanhood, and defy all else. It was stunned and stricken for the moment; but its hour of vengeance would come —vengeance on itself, and rebellion against the world.

For the wind had changed, the positions were altered; and "I am no more for Jacqueline, I am for Petronille," was written unblushingly on the Chevalier's forehead. He was a little sorry for Jacqueline; the poor little girl certainly loved him; but, pass! that would soon go. He measured Jacqueline by himself. Flow on, pleasure! flow on, caprice! He was a little volatile, he confessed it; but his Madame de Croï pleased him, and would steady him. He had been a little of a rover; but to be a lady-killer had only been reckoned a feather in his cap, rendering him all the more captivating.

No; the Chevalier was not the one man in a thousand who prefers what is nearer heaven to what is more potent on earth—" the eternal child" in Jacqueline to the worldly wisdom in Petronille. But had the question been simply that of marriage, and had a union been practicable between the cousins, Achille would have been true to his antecedents : he would not have hesitated to fulfil the family contract, and wed his kinswoman, the future Dame de Faye, though all he had of heart had been enslaved in the service of Petronille de Croï. He might even, with the shrewd calculation of his race, have decided complacently, at the very height of his passion, that Petronille would be the better mistress of his soul, Jacqueline the better wife of his hearth. Love in marriage was exacting and troublesome, while friendship was the very foundation on which to build the family structure. He might have gone on to arrange matters so well that he should spend his mornings with Petronille, and his evenings with Jacqueline ; just as Madame de Recamier must have early receptions for Chateaubriand, because the good Viscount dutifully devotes his evenings to Madame de Chateaubriand.

The Revolution had begun by complicating instead of simplifying the relations of social life,—complicating them by their very simplification. This was apparent at the Tour when the party assembled first. The want of a necessity for a demure veil of obligation thrown over the feelings,—the rare power of transferring homage directly and openly to its object,—in short, of being frankly fickle (the Chevalier did not call it false), was felt for a time, like the burden of wealth and leisure to a man who does not know what to do with them. The Chevalier was well instructed, but the necessity of honesty in love-making puzzled him; he was not familiar with honesty in that quarter. At the same time he was versatile and high spirited; he accommodated himself to circumstances, and made use of his freedom as soon as most men. The shade of embarrassment and chagrin which had clung to him in the opening hours was rapidly dissipated. His vehement admiration of his brilliant travelling companion—his devotion for her advancing with giant strides—was candidly manifested, and his privileged inconstancy rendered not impolitely, but audaciously conspicuous.

Everything implied that this transfer of homage had to do with the air of mystery which, from the beginning, pervaded the group, and spiced it with the genuine French flavour. Previously initiated eyes exchanged glances of intelligence. Eyes till recently in the dark, which did not deign to look daggers, or even to testify cool disapproval at the immediate consequences of what they acknowledged to be a forfeited bond, received the illumination, and did not conceal that they received it, as their owners trifled with étuis and took elegant pinches of snuff. The peasant Babette alone of the spectators darted furious glances at the heartlessness and shamelessness of the deed, a judgment in accordance with her different code of morals.

Jacqueline was eclipsed, slighted, and cast aside for a rival ; and she read the truth in cruel, crushing letters. She was not a fool, though she was something of a genius. She could use her eyes, and believe their testimony ; and to a French girl of rank, however young and inexperienced, the catastrophe was not altogether extraordinary. Of course the dissolution of the family contract of marriage was a strange accident; but not so Achille's short memory and the successful seductions of a rival. Jacqueline had been simple enough, in her novitiate and republicanism, not to weigh the advantages of Madame de Croï. But whenever these advantages were brought face to face with her, she recognised, with a heart grown heavy as lead, that they must win the day. Achille de Faye had need to be more than Frenchman to resist them. And Jacqueline had become aware, the moment the spell was broken, that Achille was no more than a vain, volatile, brave Frenchman in misfortune. It is in an ordinary Frenchman and Frenchwoman's nature to care for effect, even to trifling pieces of finery. Rousseau confessed to preferring a plainer woman with a prettier riband, and Montaigne to priding himself on the pearls and gold brocade of the objects of his grand passions. And in a standard modern author, a Marquise is made to defend herself for her weak-

ness in forgetting that a comedian was not a man,
even after a glimpse of his ordinary sordid squalor
had exposed it to her, and for having her cold
heart aflame for him during half a lifetime, because
she last parted from him in the white satin trunk
hose and cerise knots of Don Juan in " The
Soothsayer of the Village." There are great natures exceptions to this vanity, as there were
exceptions to the fantastic dramatic impulse which
gave a ghastly, theatrical air to so many scenes
in the Revolution ; but Jacqueline was not en-
titled to count on an exception. A choking resignation and despair, like the waters of death,
welled up and flowed over her as she crept behind the folds of the velvet curtain and hid there.
Achille was lost to her just when she had learnt to
set her heart on him. And there was no help for it:
Madame de Croï dressed so well, was so handsome
and elegant, knew so much that Achille knew, and
could display so well her repertoire. Jacqueline
was a poor, rustic gentlewoman, awkward, ignorant, stupid, well nigh imbecile. She thought the
ringing tongues, the musical laughter, and the

proud, gay faces of the pair, amidst all the distress of the world without, would drive her mad,
unless she put her fingers in her ears, and shut her
eyes hard, to keep the sound and the sight out.
Achille was lost to her; and what was left to
her at her sixteen years? There were no convents now for her to take refuge in, to turn her
back on the world and her face to God. She
would only be an incumbrance and an anxiety
to Monsieur and Madame. She wished she were
dead in her early youth.

If readers had seen Jacqueline in her lurking-
place as she revolved these miserable, dreary,
evil thoughts, they would have started at a face
such as they may have come upon occasionally
in portrait galleries, and perhaps once or twice in
actual life—a face to impress them at the time,
and still more to haunt them afterwards; a distraught young face, with eyes preternaturally large,
and waxing larger and larger under the gazer's
look.

There was one person, and only one, present
who formed a more correct estimate than her

circle of the conflicting claims of Jacqueline and
Petronille. It was not Babette; for although
she loved her young mistress dearly, and ground
her strong white teeth at this issue, she too regarded Madame de Croï as by far the finer
woman—very nearly as fine as the lady in the
caravan from Alsace. Was it wonderful that the
judge who decided in Jacqueline's favour—not
out of partiality, but in good faith—was Madame
de Faye? Monsieur the Baron might have his
doubts, bewildered and dazzled as men are liable
to be; Madame had none.

"What does the woman fear for?" she began
her reflections deliberately, apostrophising Madame
de Lussac. "Her own paltry spark of a life?
It does not merit the trouble of being blown out,
any more than that of her reader, Mademoiselle
Troche. They will soon go out of themselves,
poor women, if the people will only have patience.
She might have more to think of. What! a
daughter born a Lussac, by marriage a Croï, and
with a taint that is cousin-german to vulgarity!
Nevertheless it is so. My Jacqueline is an awk-

ward, unformed child, who may be anything yet.
The worst is, she will believe in the whole world
and embroil herself with it, like a saint in the
middle ages.   But in that there is not a shade
of vulgarity.   Petronille de Croï is like a finan-
cier's daughter : she seeks to shine, she struggles
to rule.   Ah! how low that is!   She is a liar,
in look and act, in assuming the tournure and
costume of the old régime.   We others governed
because we could not help it.   We ruled without
effort or design.   We scorned to conceal our
worst sins.   We were grand dames to the last.
For you, my Chevalier, I can follow your game.
Petronille de Croï's dot will maintain you in
exile now that Jacqueline de Faye's domain is
destined beyond remedy to confiscation.   Good.
Petronille's heart is also favourable to you, for
you will prove a better chevalier than the Marquis
to conduct her to England, and thus prevent
hazard and ennui. She may marry you. Ah!
well, I forgive you, my cousin.   Every man must
have care for himself, and the very chapter of
the Knights of Malta is dissolved. I forgive you

for everything but being actually light-headed for this Petronille's smile and favour. Chut! I hear the creaking of the joints of the young woman's mind. But men have thick heads and dull brains. They cannot always tell the pewter from the silver, or see that peacocks are not birds of paradise. They have a shade of vulgarity themselves. We are otherwise."

Madame de Faye's acute intellect and perfect taste had detected the blemish in the idol, as well as the double end in the attraction. She reigned by sheer majesty, with an airy aimlessness, and was transparent as crystal. Madame de Croï was imperious in her affability, intriguing in her fascinations, Janus-faced in her good nature. She patronized and caressed Jacqueline from time to time as " my young friend," " my darling," " my rosebud " — combating skilfully Jacqueline's hasty, harsh, reckless answers. She professed to investigate Jacqueline's accomplishments, and craved to hear her play " All along the River" on the harpsichord, and sing " He is always the same ; " and to see her paintings on velvet, and her bouquets of artificial flowers. She made Jacqueline prodigal offers of copies of " I have seen Dorinde, she smiles on me," and of whole yards of tinted velvet from her boxes, as if for the sole purpose of eliciting from the Chevalier—intoxicated with passion—extravagant compliments on her universal attainments and her generous temper. Finally, Madame de Croï rallied Jacqueline playfully, and uttered exclamations of wonder and delight at the poor girl's shyness and crossness, vowing it was celestially modest and natural; until the victim was stung to the last atom of endurance, and every word quivered in her heart like so many goads. And when Petronille interrupted the Chevalier, as he besought her, at parting for the night, to deign to remember him in her dreams, by turning wilfully to Jacqueline and insisting on embracing her, and assuring her in her voluble, honied accents, " I would love better to dream of you, my droll, my angel "—Jacqueline could have returned the kiss with a blow.

Jacqueline's first experience of grand society

ended in sharp, prostrating pain, and bitter, un-
qualified mortification. But she was wrong when
she turned away from Babette that night, twisted
her long curls into a rope, and sobbed herself to
sleep, thinking that she could never know greater
anguish. Alas! poor Jacqueline is not alone in
her dream that a girl's sentimental heart-ache can
match a woman's soul's misery. And before the
next day had well dawned she would have given
her world to return to this night's sorrow, rage,
and shame,—would have thought herself fortunate
could she have put away the new experience which
was causing her young blood to turn to gall, her
brain to reel, her heart to rise in fierce revolt
against man and God, and be again merely the
slighted, forsaken girl.

But Jacqueline's friends did not all play with
étuis, take snuff, and contemplate the course of
events with grand imperturbability. Early next
morning, before any one was astir at the Tour, ere
the white mist hanging over the landscape was dispersed by the sun, Babette, in her turkey-red gown,
and white cap, beneath which the black eyes

showed like jet, was abroad and hurrying to the
auberge.   She would have gone to early mass for a
blessing and luck, but the priest who was to re-
place Monsieur Hubert was not to arrive for a day
or two.   And she did not mind a magpie on the
branch of a walnut tree, for she was in too earnest
a mood to be turned back by trifles.   Even at that
hour, a woman was filling her pitcher at the fountain; while a few goats and a cow or two, under the
charge of a boy whistling and peeling a wand, were
drinking at the trough.   Babette nodded shortly,
but neither diverged to the right nor to the left.

She walked with nostrils distended and arms
crossed, muttering, " That monster of a fine lady !
That snake and tiger of a Chevalier !   Monsieur
and Madame would look on, and see my Mademoiselle sacrificed and eaten, poor little partridge !
—if it were done comme il faut.   What will Michel
Sart say—he to whom she is the Will-o'-the-wisp ?"
Babette's voice fell lower, and her straight brows
gloomed and contracted, till, forming three single
lines, they touched her hair on the one side and
her eyelids on the other.   " Babette has not sown

all her wild oats yet, or she would not know so
well what Mademoiselle Jacqueline must feel to be
left—Bah! Yet the little Mademoiselle would bite
her tongue out of her head before she complained.
She also is noble. Only she fled from me last
night, and she moaned as I undressed her, 'It
is my head, my good Babette; there is such an
ache there; the company has been too much for
me;' just as if the ache were not in her heart, and
as if this fine abominable Madame de Croï and
that Chevalier were not her executioners. And
Babette too is an honest girl, with a pretty little
dowry saved from the earnings of her industry.
The monkey, Citizen Pepin, would take her
even without these few golden louis, though his
superior, Michel Sart, has no mind for a good
wife that would lay down her superb hairs for a
carpet under his feet. Superior! Ouf! We are
all equals, or what good is it to women that
there is citizenship in France, tell me, then?
Not a rag. I hate it, the citizenship," stamping
her foot as she walked, "I do not care who hears
me; I can keep my head, I. King Pharamond

and serfdom again would please me.   But the play
is not played out yet.   La Sarte is a wise woman,
pure and pious as a religieuse.   All the saints in
heaven are very inconsiderate and ungrateful if
they do not listen to her prayers ; for I am sure
she does their worship credit,—infinitely more
credit than the kite Agathe, who is all stuck over
with the ugly feathers of selfishness and hypocrisy.
Perhaps La Sarte will give me some advice, some
word to say that will pierce the thick skin of
the pig of a Chevalier, or cause the soft cheek
of the proud, splendid cat, Madame, to blush.   If
Mademoiselle would only hold herself up, and
look them in the face, and answer them ! She
can chatter of books and nature, and the universe
full of the same universal sufferers—men and
women and little children,—and then her cheeks
are like the roses, and her eyes like the stars,
and she is Michel Sart's Will-o'-the-wisp.   She has
some charm, truly, my poor Mademoiselle ; she is
innocent as a dove and generous as a princess, and
I, her servant, adore her, and could die for her,
and do everything but one for her.   La Sarte may

know some harmless spell to wile that dragon of
a Chevalier back to his duty. Oh! he will be
punished sublimely if he wander away after that
dame. She is a woman of the world. She can
love him sufficiently just now, above all because
he is another's; but she will love herself the best,
and the last, and she will compel him to serve
her,—the service will be his, not hers. Excel-
lently, ravishingly, will he be paid in his own coin,
even though she treat him to no worse trick. La
Sarte may pray to some of the saints—to St.
Marthe, or St. Agnès, or my St. Barbe; they will
care more for a love-story, and feel more for a
slighted woman, than the men, like St. Audache
or St. Sulpice, if they are good for anything—the
holy saints forgive me the injury of the thought;—
they will take care that the grand lady appear as
hideous as the foibles and vices she makes so light
of. They will take care that my Mademoiselle,
who is like the good dear saints and loves them,
look as beautiful as themselves, and recall the
base heart of the man to comprehend and value
her beauty, and rush back to her, and abide by

her, and wed her, as becomes the Chevalier and the Demoiselle de Faye—behold!" With which happy conclusion Babette arrived at the auberge.

As Babette had expected, though it was not six o'clock, Maitre Michel had eaten his fricassée of kidneys, his fruit and cheese, had drunk his wine, and was gone about the business of the day. La Sarte was washing up the breakfast dishes and the solid silver spoons, in the gallery overlooking the courtyard, with the sunny mist curling off from the cheerful scene below,—at that moment astir with farm animals and servants setting out to the fields —La Sarte on her stage above the whole, as if her natural refinement had given her the pre-eminence.

Babette received a friendly welcome, and was asked to read a letter which the rural post had dropped that very morning at the auberge. The letter was from La Sarte's little son, her darling son, who had caressed her most and vexed her most, as well as made her most proud ; over whom, therefore, her heart hovered perpetually, in mingled faith and fear. It was a short, but satisfactory letter, without any sign of the 10th of

August, having been written ten days before.
Letters took long then to reach the provinces :—

"Mamma," the peasant-born deputy wrote to his
mother, "your son is commissary of one of the
sections. He would like to embrace you on his
appointment, but he cannot, so he writes instead.
How are you, our good Michel, and all the people
of Faye? Happy as angels, I hope. Salutation
and fraternity—— No, these words are not for
you: friendship and love to Faye. Were my
namesakes the jonquilles as fragrant this spring
as formerly? I had dreams of their fragrance,
and of wearing one in my button-hole. Did you
remember to put one on the altar of my Lady
every day of the season, as once on a time you
put your own kicking, screaming little diable of a
Jonquille? I am sure you did. And do you still
look at the moon, mamma, at vespers, as we said
we would look? I am very busy, but I do not often
forget. Only, corbleu! the moon is ill to find in
the narrow, dark, filthy streets of Paris. Nothing
but lamps here, mamma ; and very villanous
lamps sometimes. I saw Ambrose the other day.

He is still a journeyman baker.   But these are good days for the workmen of Paris,—for none better, except for the orators.   Ambrose is a Monsieur with silver buckles, and would cause the boys of Faye to die with envy.   Until we meet again, mamma, writes your devoted son, JON-QUILLE SART."

When Babette had paid her tribute of admiration to Jonquille's penmanship, his style, his promotion, and, what struck her less, his loving remembrance of his mother, La Sarte restored the letter to her ample pocket, and, looking into her visitor's face with the velvet eyes, which were altogether distinct from Babette's, suggested : " But what will you, Ba-bette ? " and repeated the inquiry, "Does it go quite well with you at the Tour ? " seeking a reason for Babette's morning call and the unexpressed trouble in the restless movements of the village belle.

Then, in a flow of the mouth, it all came out : what company had come to the Tour ; how it was a family affair, how Mademoiselle's business was going topsy-turvy.   Could not La Sarte, the wise woman, recommend some prescription to restore the Chevalier to his senses? Had she no nuts of King Philibert, no stones of St. Denis?

"My bue, no: I am not a sorceress," objected La Sarte, gravely; "but whether the Chevalier be brought back to his right mind or no, the good God takes care of all."

Ah! there it was. Babette sprang up, her stout figure quivering with anxiety and excitement. Would La Sarte pray to the saints, and promise them a pilgrimage, or anything in reason, if they would interfere and preserve to little Mademoiselle her rights, and break the chain which that cruel Madame de Croï was weaving; and re-establish peace and happiness at the Tour?

La Sarte, standing clear-faced and resolute in the morning sunshine, shook her head: " I love Mademoiselle; but because I love her, I would not ask these things for her,—I would not if I were you, Babette. I did not ask the stewardship for Michel, or the deputyship for Jonquille. These are motes, at best, in the broad, pure light of heaven; and, alas! they are often snares and pitfalls. They may be good if the Lord send

them of His will; but if we seek them with our
whole heart and soul, pray prayers and vow vows
for them, and weary Him with our importunity,
they turn to dust and ashes, and beget worms,
and toads, and vipers in our grasp. So is a
man's love for a woman. Does it come freely
from God and himself, with his parents' consent?
—it is her crown and her blessing. Does it
come from her own stratagems and labours?—it
is her cross and her curse. As for peace at the
Tour—is there peace in France or peace on earth,
my girl? Let peace too alight like a dove, or
like a dove depart."

"My faith, then, La Sarte," protested Babette,
sullenly, "where is the use of being so good?"

"Hold! Where is the use of Heaven, you
wicked child?" exclaimed La Sarte, indignantly.
"Where is the use of blessedness, which comes by
the pains of the holy Son of Mary first, and by our
baptism into work and sorrow afterwards? Is it
that you think we would ever ask Heaven, if we
could have earth—till we were so surfeited with
good things that we could not stir hand or foot,

or lift an eye, like so many mules? For the
rest, you are young, Babette," La Sarte relented,
"and I love you because you are the daughter of
Alix, who was confirmed with me, span and
danced in the rondes with me, was my friend and
my confidante, and helped to dress me as a bride.
And I,—I helped to dress Alix not only for the
nuptials, but for the bier. Ah! she got far before
me, at the last. Also I love you, my dear, because
you love your mistress. A faithful heart! But
leave her alone, good and clever Babette; trust
her to Heaven, as I say to our Michel. If
Heaven does not see her fit for the Chevalier,
or the Chevalier fit for her, in this stormy weather,
—why, the saints will provide her with another
husband, or keep her as safely without a husband,
my dear Babette. The good God's love can make
up a million times for the want of man's, as I
hope you will find for yourself if you have need,
little roguish Alix's sainted daughter, Widow Alix's
brave daughter. What a brave girl it is!" finished
La Sarte, contemplating Babette's broad shoulders
in the same admiring mood with which she was

in the habit of regarding her big son Michel's
stalwart proportions.

Thus Babette was forced to swallow a wholesome
draught of resignation and heavenly-mindedness,
which came home to her more fully than La Sarte
intended.   No more chance of the branch of four-
leaved trefoil to be inserted by stealth into the
bouquet of jessamine in Mademoiselle Jacqueline's
bodice; or the tiny image of St. Benedict to be
sewed surreptitiously beneath the great flap of the
Chevalier's under waistcoat.   And Babette could
have managed both performances so neatly!
Livery servants, like liveries, were abolished; so
that she would have had no fellow-servant to cajole
and bribe.

Babette found that she could not do much for
her mistress's interest, or her own.   But one little
thing she did.   She made a détour on her way
back just to carry home a cup of water from the
holy spring of Faye; and she contrived to place
the draught before the Chevalier,—drunken, but
not with wine,—as he sat next Madame de Croï.
Babette waited on them at dinner, from which

Jacqueline had begged to be excused, on the plea of attendance on her mother, who always dined in her chamber. But poor Babette! the Chevalier only glanced into the glass, and pointing to the reflection it contained, said with passion: "I drink to your image here, Madame, though it is imperfect."

"Do you hope to perfect it, Monsieur?"

Babette was so infuriated that, with singular awkwardness for a French servant, she struck against the glass in removing a dish, and spilt a great part of the water on the Chevalier's breast. If that unsound region could not be cured of its infidelity and folly, it should at least have one little bath to cool it.

"Sacré, Babette! cannot you keep the water to yourself?" cried the young man, shaking out his cambric, his dog's-ears, and his very queue.

"Good! Monsieur!" answered Babette, stiffly and sourly, like a spoiled servant, whom the times still further exempted from ceremony. "But I have no self-love; and though I serve, I am thankful I have not a beak and claws."

CHAPTER V.

THE Lussacs were to rest three days at Faye. On the second day Jacqueline was summoned to her father's room to have an interview with him. A solemn proceeding, calculated to impress her beforehand.

Monsieur's room was as unlike as possible to Madame's. It was sombre and austere; its walls were bare, except for heavy old bookcases and books; its chairs were covered with black leather. The traces of costliness were in its surgical instruments, chemical apparatus, and specimens illustrative of natural history. The last did not increase the cheerfulness of the room, for the traces of moths and the signs of decay were visible in the stuffed crocodile whose gaping jaws guarded the door, in the hook-beaked eagle on its perch by the window, and in the mysterious roc's egg hanging from the ceiling.

When Jacqueline entered, she found, to her astonishment, the whole three gentlemen of the party assembled. Monsieur sat in his chair at his bureau, supported on the right hand by the Marquis, and on the left by the Chevalier.

Jacqueline paused on the threshold, and the gentlemen saluted her. She recovered herself in a moment, saluted them in return, and passed up the room to her father with something of the grace and ease which had characterized her entrance into the auberge on the night of La Sarte's fête. Her woman's heart was beginning to burst its swaddling-bands, to flutter, to beat—to bid her put her hand on her breast and hide the wound there, to hold up her head, and smile, and die hiding it —now that she was among people who, although they were of her own grade, did not understand her, any more than did the peasant circle at Faye, and might misjudge her like them.

Monsieur took her two little hands and drew her
down to a stool beside him. For a second or
two the blood flushed over her face, and then
receded, leaving her white as a very narcisse, and
in seeming danger of swooning. In the brief
interval the thought struck her that the new
light of the last day had been an *ignis fatuus*, a
bad dream,—that Achille was about to return to
her, rather that he had never left her. But Achille
did not look at her; his head was bent, as he
traced patterns on the floor with the sword he still
wore; and the first words Monsieur spoke dis-
pelled the illusion for ever.

"My daughter, you must know that the family
arrangement for your marriage with our cousin the
Chevalier is overthrown by the national misfortunes. The Chevalier now contemplates an
alliance with the daughter of my friend Monsieur
de Lussac. I have answered for it that you have
no objection," said Monsieur, speaking in a
matter-of-fact tone, and looking at her pointedly.

"None, my father," answered Jacqueline, in perfectly audible tones,—a scarlet flush settling on her

cheek as she looked Achille full in the face with her clear, bright eyes. "My cousin, permit me to wish you and your charming future wife all happiness."

The Chevalier started and winced. Was his vanity hurt at the obliging docility with which the little girl who had adored him, resigned his name and protection? Or had he a misgiving that he was making a greater sacrifice than he had conceived? He had never seen Jacqueline so beautiful, so dignified; she would be a noble woman one day, with a more winning nobleness, if that could be, than Petronille de Croï. "I told you how much I mourned our miserable misfortunes, my cousin Jacqueline," he stammered, half rising from his seat, "but I could not save myself—" He stopped abruptly, and sank down again. That was a dubious admission to make before his future father-in-law; but a glance at the Marquis showed him he was in right honourable hands. De Lussac considered the conversation quite a family affair, at which circumstances forced him to be present, but from which his unexceptionable breeding caused

him to hold himself as much aloof as was consistent
with the need of his presence.   He was leaning
back in his chair, his eyes fixed on the roc's egg,
humming a saraband, and mentally marshalling
the coming collation.   "What could I, a poor
emigrant, do?" implored the Chevalier.

Jacqueline made no reply; there could be none
from her to such a question.   But the girl's intuitions were ripening as plants under tropical skies,
—were darting like lightning across the faults of
her education, the inexperience of her youth; and
flashing the truth vividly upon her.   She had always
recoiled from marriages of suitability; they shocked
her now.   She found out, with bitter quickness of
comprehension, "there were emigrants and emigrants," in the significant French phrase.   Emigrants in rags, giving up all, and hoping all from
the goodness of God and the justice of their cause;
and emigrants who carried their luxuries and vices
with them, would not relinquish them, sold themselves for them—mingled cynics and sybarites.
These last were the noblesse who in their exile
learned nothing and forgot nothing.   But Jacque-

line ignored all this new light—was done with Achille and his weaknesses and sins.

"I wrote that I should always remain your friend, Jacqueline. Suffer that I be your friend," begged Achille, no longer boldly, but humbly, earnestly.

"My little one," her father explained, "the Chevalier our kinsman is ready to show you his friendship by a great act of regard. My old friends the Lussacs are ready to show you their friendship. They importune me to test their fidelity and kindness; and Madame and I consent."

"What is it, papa?" cried Jacqueline, looking up intently in the noble, sardonic, but suave face, and beginning to lose her colour again and to pant like a hunted creature.

"They lead you away with them to safety and prosperity."

"Go away from you and Madame, my father! Leave you in destitution, perhaps in danger and death!" cried Jacqueline, with a sharp, indignant cry.

"Softly! It is because we are surrounded by such terrors that we send you away, my little

heart.   Do you think they would be wholesome
for a marmot like you?" declared Monsieur, with
a flickering smile.

"But you are cruel, cruel!"

"Silence! my little girl," her father warned
her. "What training will Monsieur de Lussac
imagine has been given at Faye?"

"Jacqueline," pleaded Achille, rising now and
standing manly and resolute before her, "I vow to
you that I will deal with you as a very dear and
sacred trust—Petronille will not be dearer. I will
guard your happiness and honour with my life."

"I thank you, Monsieur; I do not doubt it,"
answered Jacqueline, with the calmness of despair;
"but I see no necessity for this quitting of my
parents. If I must go, why do you and Madame
not come also, my father?"

"Jacqueline, don't be foolish, my poor girl. It
is impossible. I could not get a passport. The
Marquis's protection would not stretch to me; it
will be well if it can shelter those it is intended to
cover."

Jacqueline suddenly flung herself at Monsieur's

feet, clasping his knees and bathing them with a torrent of tears: "Permit me to stay and die with you."

Her father raised her silently; he had no answer to her demand.

Jacqueline's sobs were checked, her tears frozen at their source: "But why must I depart?"

"Go, my daughter," said her father, sternly, putting her from him with an air of displeasure, yet not unmixed with patience and tenderness; "you are undutiful; you try me; you ask reasons," was spoken reproachfully by the philosopher. "This is not a place for a Demoiselle de Faye. It is not meet that the future Dame de Faye should become the object of vile schemes and machinations. If the domain be not confiscated, or if it be ever restored from confiscation, it may be preserved to a noble family by your being beyond reach and in shelter. Do you comprehend and still hesitate, Jacqueline? The Chevalier is the next heir; he is also your nearest kinsman. Need I say that I have the fullest dependence on the faith and the loyalty of the Chevalier?" ended

Monsieur, with a generous confidence which,
after what had passed, would have been incre-
dible in any but a Frenchman.

Achille responded in a low, moved voice:
" Your confidence will not be in vain, Monsieur
my cousin."

And with these words he pledged himself
solemnly to be a faithful guardian to his young
cousin,—his former plighted wife, his love of a
week, a day.

Without doubt,—so far as sentimentally sighing
his regrets to Jacqueline when Petronille would be
arrogant and perverse; so far as borrowing Jacqueline's money, if she ever had money to lend, and
gambling furiously with it, in the intention of
retrieving his losses at play, and repaying it a
thousand-fold,—so far as these went Achille would
keep his word.

The Marquis came to life, or returned from the
visionary land of pâtés and moyennenses, to add
his argument to Monsieur's determination, and
show his cordial concurrence in the plan. " My
charming young lady, make a virtue of misfor-

tune. Honour us with your society ; we will do all
we can to render ourselves worthy of the grace.
Madame the Marquise, and my daughter Petronille, will be a mother and a sister to you. For me
and the Chevalier, we will be your very humble
servants. Monsieur your father and Madame your
mother will be content. Times may change in a
crac. The princes, and you, and me, and the
others,—we may be back at the Tour by Christmas,
bringing with us rosbif, and pudding, and portère,
my beautiful, and being up to the eyes in it,"
shrugging his shoulders with great emphasis. "But
have no fear," he finished, with a little note of
encouragement, as if he had a doubt that he might
have horrified Mademoiselle by too plain raillery,
"I shall not suffer you to starve in that rough
wilderness, if the exertions of one man—a cook
who has been crowned with some poor laurels—
can prevent it."

Every one who knew the Marquis was aware
what an amount of esprit de corps and what
prospects of exquisite eating and drinking on
the other side of the Channel lay in that speech.

"It is enough, my little one. We will it. Go to your mother." And thus Monsieur dismissed both the subject and his daughter.

Jacqueline stood before her mother like a pillar of salt—so mutely protesting, so bitter at heart.

Madame received her with nothing but congratulations, and regrets, which were the next thing to congratulations. "You are going, my Jacqueline, where you cannot even send me the news and the fashions; but it is as well, for you would have made a mess of them, giddy one. Since your marriage with the Chevalier has gone off, it is quite time to make another alliance for you. And who is there to marry here, unless goats and snipes, bourgeois farmers-general and peasant officers? There are not even 'the little ends of men' who remain to be killed in Paris—not even a convent for a girl to retire to. My faith! how the world is changed! They say it is better in England; that Westminster and Kensington are not so far amiss. And Madame de Croï has letters to my Lady Holland and my Lady Jersey. As for the Marquise, when she is no longer in terror for her sheep's head, she

will sit in her, dressing-gowns and two nightcaps
and be in terror for the ague, and whimper over the
fine climate of France, and the fine days that are
gone. But Madame de Croï—I solicit her pardon,
she will then be Madame de Faye, your near
kinswoman, — she will take you out and furnish
you with a desirable parti. The Lussacs, if they
do not find England agreeable, propose to cross to
Belgium and the country of the Rhine, where our
princes and people are. There you will be at
home, my dormouse, my woodlark."

" My mother," urged Jacqueline, with trembling
white lips, kneeling on the stool at her mother's
feet, as she had knelt at her father's, " I cannot
go with the Lussacs."

" Why not, my daughter?" inquired Madame, in
simple surprise.

" Because I was to have been the wife of
Achille de Faye," fell word by word from Jacqueline's cold lips.

" What has that to do with it?" inquired
Madame, in pure amazement. " He is to be
the husband of another woman. The first

marriage agreed upon could not be; so it is very correctly cancelled and forgotten."

"I cannot forget, my mother."

"Forget what, little one? You were not his wife, and no pure-minded demoiselle, no honest girl of the people, cherishes a particular inclination and devotion for a man, until she is his wife and the Church has blessed their union," declared Madame, dogmatically.

"Then I have not been pure-minded. Oh! forgive me, forgive me!"

Madame drew back scandalized; but though she was affronted, she was not enraged. It was very rarely that she thought it worth while to be in a passion. When she did so, she was sublime. She sat curiously inspecting her shrinking, writhing daughter. "It was not the way in my day," she said at last, haughtily. "We women thought more of ourselves; and I cannot approve of such a confession; it is indelicate, immoral, violent, revolutionary. Ah! this Revolution, what has it not to answer for?"

"I have only made it to you, mamma," mur-

mured Jacqueline, terribly abashed. " He does not know it; at least, I never said it to him. I would die before he should know it."

" Quite right, so far as it goes; but still I do not understand. When I was young," continued Madame, speaking as of something she had heard with the hearing of her ears, " I read of what was romantic and absurd in the romances of Mademoiselle Scudery. She was ugly, that Mademoiselle (though she was pure blood), ugly as a child of the pavement, a gooseherd; and her lover, Pélisson, he was ugly as his spider,—no wonder he made a pet of it! Even Madame de Maintenon, the last of the pedants, though she charmed the great King in his dotage, was a duenna, an instructress. Of their set Madame de Sevigné only was graceful or beautiful. I have heard that the great Mademoiselle was not much; but she was the granddaughter of Henry, and that was enough. I forget what I wanted to say; it was this: Mademoiselle de Scudery says of this love (as says Durfé in his *Astrea*, and the silly old romance of Gerard de Roussillon tells the same story), that it will sacrifice all for the good of the object, and rejoice in the deed. It will destroy itself, and die singing, like the swan, to promote the happiness of another. Gerard loves a princess; ah! well, he resigns her that she may become the wife of Charles Martel —queen and empress—and he the lowliest of her subjects. Petronille de Croï is not a princess, she is not even a grand dame without a ruse, an embarrassment; but she can maintain this poor boy in exile, and he can protect her, and assist her to pass the time. It is a good market. And he is caught with her as St. Lambert with Madame de Chatelet; he knows no better. But what would you, Jacqueline? that he should starve? that he should die nameless and un- known in a regiment of volunteers? for he has neither money, nor power to get him a company. Still I do not comprehend;" and Madame tapped her snuff-box.

It was true Madame had given a definition of love as it was recognised in France; but either the high platonism was overstrained and did not answer to the passionate human heart, or Jacqueline's love was not the perfection of the passion, but was a rank growth, having as much to do with youthful imaginativeness and sensitiveness as with self-denial and martyrdom. Jacqueline's suddenly blown love for her cousin Achille was very real, however; and the step to which she was being driven was maddening.

"I do not wish that he may not marry Petronille de Croï, Madame; I cannot prevent it, and I would not if I could. I hope they may be happy," asserted Jacqueline with a swelling of her white throat. "But I could not dwell with them, see them every day, be the second where I was to have been the first—their pensioner, their pupil. It would make me wicked, mad, my mother," and Jacqueline shivered till her teeth chattered.

"My poor child," declared Madame, promptly and firmly, "you are mad already; that is, your head is a little touched. You have fever, cold, megrim. You will retire to your chamber; you will have soup for the sick; you will say your prayers. To-morrow you will be better, though feeble ; be in your senses, obedient, amiable, my little kitten. All these fancies will be gone ; all this talk is but a fancy. I see it now. At last I comprehend. There will be no more of it. You must command your body ; it is the forte of us, the nobles. For Monsieur and I, we will it, my daughter. We know what is good for your honour and your happiness. You go, with the last remnant of our class, to safety and society, in dull, prosperous England."

Jacqueline threw up the selfish protest ; but she continued to cling to her mother's knees, as she had clung to her father's : " Leave you, my mother, my father, never !" she cried, as she had cried to Monsieur, hoping to strike an answering chord in their breasts, and not seeing that their sentiments of parental duty and their affection for their child were her worst enemies, were what clenched her fate. " What will you do without me, mamma ? You will be so sad without your child."

But Madame would not own to weakness, to anything so bourgeois as family attachment. "Not at all, if I am satisfied on your account. It is the

law of society and of nature.   After all, Nature
is more accommodating than people think.   She is
belied, that poor woman.   The young go, the old
remain.   Agathe suffices for my toilette, and I
shall not miss you, my lamb.   You are even a
poor unpicker, my Jacqueline ; you could not earn
your bread in that way.   I have known dames,
who staked a hundred louis on one card, very glad
to earn a few thousand francs a week as unpickers.
Besides, the threads get more entangled now, and
the gold looks red, as if the lace had been in battle.
It has been in the wars many a time ; I have
detected here the black smoke of the cannon, and
there a rent and a crimson stain.   I have said
to myself, 'This was done at Verdun ; and that at
Fort-du-Quesne ; and here again a brave soul went
out.'   But to offer the poor thread for sale now,
when one pretends to forget all but frieze coats,
would be to have all our clothes dabbled crimson
together, and all our hairs shorn by the mob razor
of France."

"Let me die with you, my mother," moaned
Jacqueline.

"Not when I command you to live for me, my child," negatived Madame, with her stately tone of divine right. "Go, and send Babette, and I shall instruct her how to put up your boxes. That the Demoiselle de Faye should have no more decent trousseau, that is my grief, my little one."

Jacqueline went anew with feet that did not feel the parquetted floor, and brain that swam.

Madame looked after her only child and drew a little sigh. "Poor little one, she would always believe everything and everybody,—herself amongst the rest; and she was so inquisitive, she would not be kept in the dark, as girls should be. That sympathy,—it is a dangerous commodity. I feel myself deranged with listening to her delirium. But how? She must submit; it is for us, the quality, to submit. The Queen would be at Versailles now, and not in the Temple, if she had submitted to the exigencies of her rank. It is for me to provide Jacqueline with an example." Madame gave another little sigh, and her glance strayed to the recess where were her aids to devotion, but where, Monsieur the Curé not being to her mind, she could not be devout according to rule.

The next person Jacqueline met—and it was by chance—was Madame de Croï, whom she encountered on the grand staircase. Jacqueline's beautiful, triumphant rival stopped and hailed her with enthusiasm: "My rosebud, my stepdaughter, is it not? Ah, we will not quarrel, Jacqueline! You do not think I care because you were destined for Achille? My dear, these things are done in the cradle; and if I had a daughter I should settle her fate then, and trust that no revolution would come to unsettle it. But it will be my endeavour to find you a brilliant fortune —a bridegroom without reproach, such a one as you merit. You do not think me too young to be your chaperone? Hold! if Monsieur de Croï had possessed a daughter, say, would she not have been much older—fit to be my mother, very likely? Well, I should have been very amiable to her if she had allowed me." Petronille pinched Jacqueline's cheek meaningly, and passed on.

Jacqueline went her way, sick at the perfumed, flattering words, and not caring much whether the promise would be fulfilled. Undoubtedly Petronille would not beat or starve her, or lock her up. She would even exert herself for the promotion of Achille's cousin, unless Achille's cousin threatened to eclipse her,—an absurd supposition. She might tickle her, delicately poke her, and laugh at her, as she had done ever since the two came together. She might try to get Jacqueline's heart into her skilful hands, to dissect and galvanize it, anatomy of all kinds being much in fashion. She might, like the eruption of a flower-draped volcano, burst out on her with a torrent of fierce, bad words, when she was in one of her furies. All at once, some fine day, after seven years' acquaintance and fondling, she might play the traitor with a smile on her lips, to serve a friend, or injure an enemy, or only punish a slight offence. But eruptions do not happen frequently even in volcanic countries; and no clever woman will betray her neighbour except as a rare indulgence. Jacqueline might therefore live long

and never know those traits in Petronille's character.

Jacqueline thought little of that particular
danger. Her difficulty was how to live out the
next two days, which had shone so sunnily in
anticipation; how to live the after life, the strange,
mocking, dreary farce which seemed to stretch
into an eternity beyond. She could scarcely
tell how she spent the first of the days. By
tacit consent she was left to herself. Monsieur
and Madame did not dream of anything so hein-
ous in their daughter as obstinate resistance to
their sovereign will. Therefore, in their good
manners, in their softer relentings, they did not
persecute her with lectures and censures. Jacqueline, with due attention to the ceremonial of
society, flitted about very much as on other days,
in the places which within two sunrises and sunsets
(nay, within one), were to see her face no more, for
many a dark, troubled, and awful week and month.
She was chained to her stake at meals and at the
evening receptions; for it was not lawful that she
should absent herself from the circle of noble ladies

and gentlemen, or go out of sight and hearing of the sparkling, ardent wooing of the Chevalier, and the occasional courteous and gentle words he remembered to speak to his old love: "We will have fine weather for our journey, my beautiful cousin;" or, "Shall I write on Nerina's collar, 'I am Nerina, the dog of Citoyenne Jacqueline Faye, of the party of Citoyen Lussac.'" Worse still, she had to bear the condescending raillery and the ostentatious kisses of Petronille de Croï. No wonder that she was wild; the wonder was that she was not mad outright, as Madame had alleged in her defence.

At other hours she wandered up and down. She took counsel of all the familiar faces and scenes, but all caused her to beat her breast and hang her head in deeper despair. Paul screwed up a more vinegar face than ever at the little Mademoiselle's loss of a husband; her departure but added to his rheumatism. Agathe, who had never been fond of young girls in the Tour, fell into more foldings of the hands and Credos, as if to insinuate that the being chasséd from the Tour was a judgment on Jacqueline's transgressions, and on all the sins in which she had giddily and presumptuously abetted the insolent Babette. And Babette was the worst of the three.   Actually she seemed to have gone crazed.   She was incessantly pulling out the drawers in Mademoiselle's room, and pushing them in again; snatching up robes, jupons, and hoods, and flinging them away; abasing herself, as if she could grovel and kiss Jacqueline's feet; holding out her arms, and beseeching her Mademoiselle to fling herself into them, rest her weary young head, and cry her poor heavy eyes to sleep on her Babette's fond bosom. Babette's rich brown complexion had grown in these few days to a dun chalk colour, with patches of purple about the cheek-bones.   Her lace cap was pushed to the extreme crown of her head; the crushed lappets swung round, and hung down her back.   Her work caused her to sweat and groan almost like Agathe.

Meantime the preparations for the journey went on.   Already Jacqueline's great chest was half filled.   It was studded with brass nails, and had been at the wars with Monsieur, when he was a grey musketeer. It had seen Minden, perhaps Rosbach; and later service still, for it was not altogether free from the mould and clay it had contracted in the garden, where it had been buried with the spare plate, and only dug up that its contents might deck the buffet and table in honour of the Lussacs; and because it would be useful to Mademoiselle.

Not a single idea of resistance to the cruel command did Babette put into Jacqueline's head; not a hint did she give, in all her spasms and convulsions, to dissuade her young mistress from her unnatural destination. Jacqueline found no refuge with Babette; so after gazing at her with piteous eyes till Babette went into hysterics, she instinctively withdrew from her humble friend, and acknowledged, mournfully, that she, too, had failed her in her tribulation.

Up and down paced the restless feet, the wet eyes looking wistfully at the tapestry on the dingy mouldering walls. It represented Agamemnon and Iphigenia. Would that her

father had been another Agamemnon, and had
bound and laid her on a sacrificial altar, instead
of bidding her be gay, travel the world with Achille
de Faye and Petronille de Croï; and witness
all their confidences and caresses, after she had
seen the ceremony solemnized which would unite
the two—one of whom had been her hero, her
lover, her promised husband. French couples,
let the bond be never so slight or formal, have
always their polite confidences, their stereotyped
caresses.

Jacqueline questioned the pictures of those who
had gone before her and borne their crosses,
with her strained, weary eyes. They told her the
same tale; they all looked at her just as did the
picture of her mother. The proud, spirituelle
woman was represented as a wood nymph in
spotted leopard skin and buskins; with an ala-
baster bow in her hand, and a crescent on her lofty
unruffled brow. That picture indicated Madame
truly. Jacqueline could look back and remember
old friends of the family—Messieurs in houppe-
landes and cloth canons and curious wigs, whom

Madame called "my shepherds," and who constantly addressed her as "my quite beautiful," "my
all graceful," "my queen of queens."   But to none
of these high-flown, antiquated adorers, any more
than to Monsieur, had Madame unlocked the
secret chambers of her spirit and submitted as
to a conqueror.   Her mother's eyes, from that
picture, scorned Jacqueline for her want of intre-
pidity and magnanimity, her anguished self-
questioning, her frantic child's wailings.   Before
no figure there could Jacqueline throw herself
and ask commiseration—except before the carved
figure on His cross of Him who died for a world's
sins, and endured a world's woes.   Even here the
girl was beaten back and found no rest; for here,
beyond every place in the world, the horror of
great wickedness assailed her.   The impulse to
hate Petronille; ay, even to hate Achille, while
she loved him too with a fierce love, — that
impulse, which her scared conscience, her womanly modesty, her whole nature standing up and
fighting against it to the death, told her might
lead her to crime and remorse, was most repug-

nant and horrible here, as it seized her, threw her
down, and tore her. It was in some respects a
lying spirit; for had Jacqueline trodden that
path of most artificial yet most deadly peril,
none dare say that she might not have trodden
it safely. But her faith did not compass the
power and the love of Heaven; and there rose
up before her, in the vivid colours in which
Dante painted his hell, Monsieur Hubert's sermon
at the churchyard gate, and his warnings of the
lost women, to whom might be joined tens of
thousands more from the mighty, the noble, and
the wise.

Where should she seek refuge? At intervals
the storm in which she was struggling became
so appalling, that it seemed as if, in its very
force, it was relenting and undoing its work.
It seemed as if it would stupify and deaden
every nerve and feeling, and make her from that
moment an automaton, a cold, white, careless
girl, who would henceforth mind nothing, regret
nothing, decline nothing, but eat, drink, laugh,
and die without any more pain or trouble. These

moments were when Jacqueline was in the hall,
or in Madame's room, or promenading the terrace
and planting orange trees to celebrate the visit,
with the rest of the party. It was in one of
these moments, when there was a singing in her
ears which prevented her hearing in memory the
now hushed song of the nightingale, or in fact
Achille and Petronille's vows, and when her
heart was beating with a dull, sullen sound, as if
it were a hammer striking an anvil, muffled, to
make melancholy music, that Jacqueline committed the great blunder of her young life, the
blunder which, like the additional straw that broke
the camel's back, delivered her over for the time
to frenzy and madness.

She was conscious of her father's watching her
with scrutinizing eyes. She believed, in her dis-
traction, that he was studying her passive grief
and humiliation, as she had known him practise
surgical operations on animals, and diseased or
dead men and women, — not to relieve human
misery, like Monsieur the Curé, but to acquaint
himself with the mortal frame, and to pry into

life's mechanism, just as he had investigated the elements of matter, or interrogated philosophy and religion with the idle, never-satisfied, and for-ever-doubting question of Pilate, "What is truth?"

This morbid, aimless curiosity was one of the evil symptoms of France at the time. It neither regarded reverence, charity, nor tenderness, but invaded the holiest sanctuaries, and treated their altars as common and unclean. It frittered away the heart of man by depriving him of the old heroic capability to cut the Gordian knot of existence with the sword of duty, to carve out for himself a man's honest work and reward, and have done with this ball of earth after he had played a man's part on it, leaving the rest to God, if he were so happy as to believe in God.

But Jacqueline was never guilty of a sadder mistake than when, with the wayward, diseased ingenuity of misery, she misinterpreted Monsieur's notice of her. He was merely saying to himself, "Poor little one, better that your heart

should be broken,—young hearts mend again,—
than that you should fall into the hands of these
demons, be polluted, my virgin, or pour out your
sweet blood like water." And the infatuated child
thought Monsieur was taking stock of her woe,
making trade of it, softly pulling it about with
pincers, employing their sacred relationship to increase his familiarity with that strange animal
man, in the idiosyncrasy of his own daughter, as
ancient artists perfected their arts by observing
the agonies of slaves.

Her mind unhinged by this last ghastly miscon-
ception, Jacqueline, in a rash moment, shaped
her future destiny to its distorting light. She
slept as all young creatures sleep, that they
may rise and buckle on their loads, and become
perfect through suffering. But she woke so early
that not even her maid on the truckle bed in the
ante-room was stirring. Babette's preparations for
slumber had certainly been peculiar. She had
tilted the mattress so that the place for the heels
was higher than that for the head; she had flung
out the pillows, and where they should have been

there was a crushed bandbox, with the débris of working materials—whalebone, buttons, agraffes, even needles and pins, with stalks and stones of fruit, and crumbs of bread from her pockets, all strewn over the uneasy couch, so that she appeared rather to be doing penance than seeking repose. But she was young too, and was exhausted by her exertions of the preceding day. So there she lay, her strong arms above her head grasping the ragged edges of the bandbox, her mouth wide open, and breathing stertorously.

Jacqueline had another long day to suffer, and then the dreadful to-morrow. It might have been thought that she would have cowered down, covered her head, and shut out the light in her wretchedness. On the contrary, she got up at once, and proceeded to dress herself quickly, not so much like a victim distraught, as like a person mastered by a tyrant resolution. She did not call Babette, she scarcely looked at her as she went noiselessly out. Something, she did not stop to consider what, had cooled her heart to her maid, notwithstanding her distress of the preceding day. Was it that Jacqueline did **not** believe it genuine? that in the new suspiciousness aroused within her, she thought Babette had been suborned, gagged, induced to hang back from her, and let her go? Or was misery already rendering her callous?

Jacqueline did not tarry even at Madame's door. She quitted the tourelle and the Tour while the whole house was buried in sleep, and the shadow on the sun-dial was so short, that it was but **a** black speck. She traversed the terrace, and going round to the back of the Tour, let herself out by a wicket gate into the bocage, close behind **the** gentilhommière.

In the dense dew of the August morning twig and blade were dripping wet. The solitude **was** complete, except for Jacqueline's little lion **dog** Nerina, which had detected the light sound **of** her footstep, risen up from her wicker cradle, **and** trotted after her. Half republican as Jacqueline was, she had never gone out into the bocage, or roamed beyond the terrace, without **Babette**, any more than the Demoiselles **de** St. Cyr had

walked abroad unattended. But now she was
neither frightened for Red Riding-hood's wolf,
nor for the diabolical Monsieur, of whom that
perfidiously cruel animal was the fit emblem, as
the glittering - eyed old French bonnes stoutly
maintained.

Nerina, unaccustomed to the silence, which was
not even broken by the songs of birds, and having
her mane draggled, and her fine curls made thin,
lank, and disconsolate as candle-wicks,—Nerina,
trained to be as particular about her curls as a
petit-maitre about his wig, and spoiled into pee-
vishness, began to howl her discomfiture and dis-
gust. Being a French dog she howled, where an
English dog would have whined.

Jacqueline lifted the pampered favourite, wiped
her feet mechanically, and carried her a hundred
yards into the wood; then, standing still, she
prepared to put the dog down again, but first
she unclasped the collar which Achille had amused
himself the previous evening by furnishing with an
inscription,—" I am Nerina, the dog of Citoyenne
Jacqueline Faye. I belong to the party of Citizen

Lussac, bound with a viséed passport for Calva-
dos, thence to England." Jacqueline cast the
collar intemperately into a thicket of broom;
then looked into Nerina's silly eyes, gave her a
long, light hug, as if she represented other than
herself, and set her softly down on the moss and
leaves. The dog, finding herself once more exposed to damp and dirt, howled twice or thrice
dismally; then, taking into her own hands her
rescue from the unbecoming circumstances, she
turned tail and scampered home. A dog of
quality could not follow Jacqueline in the way
she was going.

Hares ran across her path, owls hooted from
the hollow trunks of the decayed trees, but she
held on along the footpath into which the wide
road through the Ravine of Plums had diminished.
She was not retarded, like Nerina, by the water
which the clumps of eglantine, honeysuckle, privet,
box, and tall walnut and chestnut trees, shook
down upon her in drenching showers. Soon her
clothes were clinging to her limbs, while her
streaming curls were straight as Nerina's, and

glistened with countless drops, better representing heavy tears than sparkling diamonds.

But she had reached her destination—a clearing in the wood, where a few days before she had seen Michel Sart marking some of the gigantic beeches, the pride of the old De Fayes, now sentenced to the woodman's axe. Here her fitful mind conjured up a great contrast :—the Chevalier walking beside her jauntily, courting her triflingly, touching her lightly, as a thing which belonged to him, to take or to leave at pleasure; and Michel Sart, with his leonine face all moved as she entered his mother's auberge; his bashful lips pressed like a devotee's to her chain; his reverential walk with her to the conciergerie, as her champion and defendant, not dreaming of being her equal.

If there was a human being in the world who could do anything for her it was Michel Sart. If there was a human being who would risk everything for her, it must still be this same Michel Sart.

She dropped down on the root of a tree in the chill, shady place which the sun had not yet penetrated and lighted up; where the lizards were

still below the stones, and the dragon-flies in the
loops of the long grass.   There she sat perched
like a white dove ; for, poor child ! she was all in
white, as if dressed for the service of the Virgin.
She had not half an hour to wait.   Maitre Michel's
big figure came swinging along leisurely in the
opposite direction.   She did not give him time
to discover her ; she started up, flew to him, and
clasped her hands before him.   Her moorland
eyes had assumed the look which such eyes are
said to take when excited or angry : the sparkling
pupils became detached, and seemed to strike like
balls.

"Maitre Michel, save me ! I have come to
you.   Be my deliverer.   And if that is impossible,
I say to you, kill me ; I know you will put me
out of pain gently."

He stood thunderstruck.   He thought the whole
scene was a phantasm, that his brain was on fire,
and that he was no longer qualified for any place
but a cell in a *God's-house*, in consequence of
his insane passion for Monsieur's daughter.   Even
after he had recovered himself, and could believe

his eyes, Jacqueline, draggled and dishevelled as she was, was not simply Mademoiselle to him, but an angel.

Michel Sart had heard something of Jacqueline's immediate departure with the Lussacs, and putting that and her betrothal to the Chevalier together, he had settled (though a rumour had also reached him that the family alliance was to be relinquished) that the marriage in which he was so much interested would be celebrated speedily, probably as soon as the travellers had reached a secure spot,—in some foreign ambassador's chapel, or by an emigrant priest in a private house. And this conviction was a death-blow to any selfishness in his worship.

But as it happened, he had not apprehended the true bearings of the case, for, notwithstanding all, here was Mademoiselle come to him in the deepest sorrow.

Only one thing was clear, and it was soothing and thrilling beyond description to the true, long-suffering heart: Mademoiselle came to him, she asked him to help her. "What is it, my Made-

moiselle ?   But   compose   yourself ;   trust   me.
What ails you, my young lady ?   Saints ! how **wet**
you are ! You will get your death of cold.   Come
back to the Tour ; let Babette make a crackling fire
instantly."

"No, Michel, never !   I   will   never   go   back
unless you can save me.   I say to you, Michel,
kill me with one blow, but do not send me back."
And then she told her story, sobbing and wringing
her hands, and supporting herself on her servant's
arm : how Monsieur and Madame were sending
her away ; how she did not care whom the Chevalier married, but she could not dwell with him and
Madame de Croï; how nobody felt for her; and
how even some, who ought to have cared for her,
philosophised, and entertained themselves with her
sufferings.

Michel Sart wiped his forehead as he sustained
her tenderly. "Have patience, my Mademoiselle.
Perhaps you deceive yourself.   It is to me incre-
dible.   Madman ! robber ! villain !"   It was a
bewildering light that broke on Michel Sart in the
hollow of the bocage, in the cool silvery blue of

the morning—a terrible temptation that met him there. And it was all the more terrible that he could not tell how far the strange chances of these times made it lawful for him to protect Jacqueline from what appeared wicked injury and insult, or how far it would be possible for him to deliver her from the darkening perils of the advancing Revolution, without yielding to the temptation.

"Mademoiselle Jacqueline," he said, "I would die for you with all my heart; but my dying would do you no good. You would only feel the want of me to watch over you and wait upon you." Maitre Michel hesitated, and his voice fell. He was manly and modest; he recoiled from the notion of taking advantage of her and wounding her afresh; he did not know how he could explain himself. "Mademoiselle, do you not remember that I am only the aubergiste's son and Monsieur's registrar?" he whispered, hurriedly.

"Yes, yes, Maitre Michel; but I have nobody save you," wept Jacqueline, inconsiderately and incoherently, "and I thought you would do something for me."

"But do you not see there is only one way?" he panted.

"What way?" cried Jacqueline, with asperity. "O Sainte Dame! make him tell it me."

"I dare not tell it; you will lose all confidence in me; you will hate and despise me," Michel protested, vehemently.

"No; a hundred times no. I said, 'Kill me, but don't suffer me to go back and be carried away by those people there.' I will rather die here, when I am innocent, and everybody will be sorry for me, and the good God will pardon me, because I asked for death rather than that the demons should reign in my heart, and I live to be vile. Women have died in the Revolution already; women are lying in crowds in the prisons of Paris. Oh! these are times of lamentation. Whatever it is, I will bless you, Michel Sart."

"I cannot kill you, Mademoiselle; it would not be like killing myself. I do not think anything could make me kill you, unless it were to put you beyond horrible wrong and suffering," declared Michel, with desperate determination. "The angels guard you from these, though you have known that life is hard! But—see you—I could marry you,—forgive me for saying it,—and Monsieur could not send away my wife. No other interference on my part is possible."

Jacqueline stared at him blankly and confusedly. It was not at all what she had expected. Such a step was so entirely out of her calculations that the alternative had not crossed her mind. Whatever irregularities were in France, mésalliances, in spite of Voltaire's Nanine, were hardly known. Very few had recourse to such solutions of the strife between Aristocrat and Republican, even when marchionesses worked as day-labourers on humane farmers' fields, and countesses cooked in soft-hearted bankers' kitchens. Where the ancient virtues of purity, fidelity, and loyalty were often looked upon as bourgeois, the conventionalities still prevailed with an iron rule ; and when they were broken, the iron entered into the soul of the offender.

Jacqueline's wan face crimsoned, and then grew paler than ever. She covered her face with her hands. "What is this that I have done?" Then, with her noble forbearance and consideration for the feelings of others, she blamed herself and spared him, at the same time deciding her fate. The consideration that it was she who had compromised Michel Sart, and impelled him to his proposal, had great influence over her in this decision. "Michel Sart," she said, extending her hand to him, "in any other circumstances it would not have been fit that you should have spoken such words, or that I should have listened to them; but I forced you to say them,—I, who am a miserable, humiliated, distracted girl. I am not worthy of you, Michel Sart, except for the rank which I have forgotten in coming here to you. I pray you to think twice before you repeat your words. One man has resigned me; I will not take another man, whoever he may be, by surprise, and induce him to sacrifice himself, to put me in shelter.——What! you would still have it so? Then, Michel Sart, take me, and hide me as your wife; it is an honourable title; I will forget that I have borne any other."

He did not thank her, he did not oppress her with his secret joy; he would still have thought it sacrilege to let her have a glimpse of it. But neither did he charge her to pause and count the cost, as she had bidden him : he felt the time for that was past ; it was too late. Whatever Jacqueline forgot, neither could ever forget these words in the solitary wood. In his position of her father's retainer, he could no longer continue to shield his young lady. He had crossed the Rubicon : he must be everything to her now, or nothing.

Michel Sart, though by nature a slow man, made the necessary arrangements for executing their purpose rapidly ; and he made them, on this the most exciting morning in his life, with fore-thought and exactness. He took Jacqueline down with him through the plum ravine to the hamlet. The late flowers of July were all withered, and the plums plucked, while the blackberries and nuts were not yet ripe. No birds sang, and no little girl sang with them,—

" If Henry should offer me his Paris,
I would not quit my dear, O gué !"

No gallant Chevalier clapped his jewelled hands, and looked with kind looks at his plighted bride. No Babette encored rapturously. But Jacqueline scarcely glanced around to miss what she had lost. When she did, it was ·with lacklustre eyes.

Maitre Michel was compelled to leave Jacqueline at the mouth of the ravine, as he went his way through the still quiet village street to the auberge. She, dreading detection, and shivering with more than cold, stood watching the light blue smoke from the charred-wood fires which began to curl out of the holes that served for chimneys in the cottage roofs, and listening to the hoarse bark of a dog of the people, very different from the treble yelp of Nerina. But Maitre Michel was not gone many minutes, when he returned in one of those seated charrettes in which country people go to market, with a strong work-horse yoked between the trams.

It did occur to Jacqueline: "Oh, I wish he had brought La Sarte, a woman like myself, a good woman. She might have told me if I avoid

misery by committing an inexpiable crime. My
parents chase me away. Assuredly I am but anti-
cipating their wish in thus cutting myself off for
ever from them and the Tour." But she did not
say out what was passing in her mind; and Michel
had not spoken to La Sarte, it would have troubled
him to tell why.

Ah! as Jacqueline said, if he had only brought
La Sarte. Old eyes see so much farther; old
heads, grown hoary in virtue, are in a sense like the
little children, so much nearer heaven. But though
Michel Sart had not brought his mother, he had
brought her great red market cloak and hood to
wrap and muffle Jacqueline in, and wine and bread
to sustain her.

But Jacqueline's veins were already throbbing
with fever and false strength, and there was danger
in delay.

"I am so sorry that I have nothing better,
Mademoiselle," said Maitre Michel, as he lifted
into the peasant's cart the girl who had only
ridden in an allegorically painted, velvet lined
aristocrat's coach.

"Oh! do not think of it," Jacqueline said sincerely. "It is to me all the same,"—and so indeed it would have been, had she had to trudge along the road till she fell with fatigue, or mount a tumbril amidst the familiar attitudes and expressions of the members of her class. Only the sight of the axe, or the platoon of soldiers, or the rapid rushing river, would have aroused her with a shock and a pang. And then she might have measured the trifling vantage-places of this world by the starry heights above her; her past life might have lain mapped out behind her, as it shows to a drowning man; and she might have seen again with clear eyes and spoken again with a fluent tongue.

To accomplish a marriage between these two citizens, it was necessary that Maitre Michel, ere their folly could have a chance of being discovered, should convey Jacqueline to the next town of La Maille, and stand with her before the mayor, marriages being already ordained civil institutions. After signing the contract, it depended upon the private sentiments of the couple whether they would then have recourse to a priest, and add the Church's authority and blessing to the bond.

The Demoiselles de Faye, Jacqueline's ancestresses, had walked in a circle of nobles, over flower-strewn paths, and in sweeping brocades, to the village church or the family chapel, there, kneeling before gold-crowned, incense-streaming altars, to take the sacramental vows from the lips of bishops and archbishops. But Jacqueline was jolting along a rough road in a peasant's cart, shrouded in an aubergiste's cloak. She was journeying in the secrecy of the dawn, to appear like a thief before a mayor, with her father's servant for her bridegroom,—and all because she could not conduct herself as if she had neither conscience, memory, nor heart, as became her rank.

Michel Sart did not intrude himself on his mistress's attention. He was a quiet man at all times, a good listener, speaking to the point what he did say, and only dealing with the heart of a matter. And his mind might now misgive him sorely; the wonderful acquisition of his treasure might well be grievously overshadowed. The mocking fiend " Too late !" while it urged him on, might even now taunt him horribly. " False servant to Monsieur," it might cry ; " usurper and invader of aristocratic rights, though the Assembly has decreed all men equal ; strong man profiting by a girl's weakness."

It was Jacqueline who spoke occasionally, and what she did say was as if there was nothing extraordinary in the scene and the position of the actors : merely a dry remark on the pasturage, "It has need of rain, has it not, Maitre Michel ? " or on the vineyards, " The National Guard must be set free to gather the grapes ;" or on the low hills bordering the horizon, " Are these the Côtes de Bruyére ? " as if she were speaking in a dream. And Jacqueline had not been a dozen times so far from home in her whole previous history.

The sun was shining full on the walls of the old town, on its single square and its few dependent streets, its narrow houses with projecting upper stories, broad spouts, and tiled roofs indented like finger-nails.

There was no stoppage at the gate, where

Michel, who was well known, was hailed by the officers : "Good day, citizen, and a good market. Peste ! the market is not till to-morrow ; you are a day in advance, citizen !"

Inside the gate were great fortified dwellings, with coats of arms above the doors, more frowning and formidable than the Tour de Faye. Happily Jacqueline knew nobody here, but she gazed up at the great houses, her thoughts recurring to home : " They will have missed me at Faye. They will be searching up and down ; Babette the wildest. They think I have been a great sinner, and that I have plunged into the Mousse at Gaspard's mill-dam. I am a great sinner, and it will be all the same to them as if I had drowned myself. But you could not help it, Maitre Michel; so do not think of it," Jacqueline begged him, with the exquisitely fantastic courtesy of her high breeding.

Michel guided the charrette to the most re-tired inn ; but even it had proclaimed itself an auberge of the Nation, and raised a red cap for a sign. He did not ask for a private

room, because that would have subjected Jacqueline, without the armour of assurance or experience,
to the curiosity, cross-questioning, and suspicion of
the sharp landlady while he was absent making
the necessary arrangements.   But he and his companion had the best seats at the table in the porch.

There sat with them a screaming politician of
course, a soldier in a grey coat, and a market-
woman, with heavy gold rings on her thick brown
fingers.   The last glanced more stolidly than
wrathfully at Jacqueline's small white hands,—her
face being shaded by La Sarte's hood,—and at her
soiled, crumpled white gown.

"And how goes the hemp and the flax this year
over at Faye, Maitre Michel?   Oh, you were the
wise man to turn farmer instead of aubergiste before
the roads were blocked up : not but that the
Nation is a fine thing,"—the hostess corrected herself, diplomatically,—" and the nationalists always
thirsty ; but we need all strings to our bow,—you
comprehend, Maitre Michel?   The Citoyenne eats
nothing," concluded the good woman, in a little
tone of offence at the slight to her soup.

"The Citoyenne is indisposed," Michel put her off.

"My gossip has eaten her chickens in place of bringing them to market," observed the market-woman jocosely, stopping, with her mouth full of fried potatoes, to point to her own well-filled basket.

There was a laugh, for they were all in good humour, although the politician kept vociferating, mechanically, "No rents, no domains; let brothers share acre by acre. If not, to the lamp-post, or to the new Madame Guillotine, with every mother's child of the aristocrats."

But Jacqueline trembled and quailed through her stupor. She was not yet insensible to the love of life, though she had bidden Michel Sart kill her, thinking that she preferred death to her frenzy of abasement and poignant pain. She crept close to Maître Michel; and, through all his gnawing care and self-reproach, it was sweet as heaven on earth to have her pressing close to him. But even while he tasted the sweetness, Michel Sart remarked a gaunt-visaged, spectacled man in the long coat of a priest, with the box of a pedlar on his back, entering the inn. He quitted Jacqueline for a minute, and interchanged one or two words with the stranger. "He will do our business, Mademoiselle," he whispered, on his return, "when we are done with Monsieur the Mayor. He is the successor of Monsieur Hubert. I guessed it. He does not care what we are, but he has asked me if there are any bookstalls in the town; and I fancy also he is carrying a small library on his mule, and that he is his own mule when his beast feeds, lest any scholar run off with his books." Michel ran on in this light fashion, for him, glad of any refuge from his own thoughts. "Without doubt he will be very orthodox. Look up and see how he puffs under the Fathers. Will he take them into the church of St. Laure, which is now standing open, a home for mendicants, and where no curé will interfere with us? Does it please Mademoiselle?"

"As you will," answered Jacqueline, wearily.

It was only a step from the auberge to the mairie, and Jacqueline traversed it with La Sarte's hood pulled down over her face, and clinging to Michel Sart's strong arm. The mairie was just opened, and two or three clerks were sauntering across the whitewashed room, whistling and staring. Monsieur the Mayor was not so devoted a public servant that he relished being disturbed at his omelette and pickled herring (his mother was from Alsace) to celebrate a marriage. At first he sent word that the couple must wait. But when he was told they could not wait, and was reminded that it was business hours, he appeared unceremoniously with a napkin round his neck, resolved to dispose of the affair as quickly as possible, and return to his unfinished meal.

" Monsieur the Mayor, I have the honour to ask you to celebrate a marriage between me, Michel Sart, registrar to Citizen Faye, and Citoyenne Jacqueline Faye, ci-devant Demoiselle de Faye, and to permit two of your clerks to be witnesses to the contract," said Michel, firmly.

Monsieur the Mayor stared. He had inherited more than the taste for pickled herring from his Alsacian mother. He was solid and phlegmatic for a Frenchman, and this morning there was a call for despatch in his duties. But Michel Sart, though known at the auberge and the gate, and generally in La Maille, was not known to the mayor, who, though a republican, was an honest man, and the father of daughters.

"I do not see the face of the Citoyenne. We are not accustomed to marry cloaked and hooded brides," objected he, suspiciously.

A listlessness and numbness had stolen over Jacqueline's faculties in spite of her fever; but she heard enough to aid Michel when he uncloaked her. Poor little girl! what a wretched object she was in the draggled white gown, the train of which had been pulled out of the pocketholes, had been rent and trodden upon, and now hung like a tattered banner half a yard behind her. How the clerks of the mairie shrugged their shoulders and marvelled! Still the white dress was bridal-like, and the dull trouble and panic in her face caused her to look years older.

"Do you consent, of your free, true will, Mademoiselle—— ahem!—Citoyenne? Both con-

tracting parties must fully consent," floundered
the mayor, as a precaution.

"Is it I?—I consent? It was I who made
the marriage," said Jacqueline, candidly, regarding the mayor with her great eyes.

"Pardi! that is more than I bargained for. I
asked if you consented, not if you originated the
alliance; but it is all the same thing,—that is,
if the Citizen consents, of which I presume there
can be no doubt," ended the mayor, with more
of a sneer than a gallant compliment.

His insinuation pointed to some villany. And
taking the wild looks and the admission of the
girl, in connection with the mute testimony of
Michel Sart's manly, trustworthy bearing, he very
likely settled that it was villany to be covered and
atoned for, rather than to be begun by this ceremony. Still it was not the part of a magistrate to
refuse to perform a legal rite.

A formal question and answer, and the reading
of a paper, to which Michel signed his name,
plain "Michel Sart," in the big, bold characters,
not of a peasant, but of a soldier, and to which

Jacqueline appended her signature in the fine, aristocratic Italian hand of all the demoiselles of her generation,—"Jacqueline Bertrande de Faye,"—and the work at the mairie was done. The deed was like the letter which Jacqueline had written in her chamber to the Chevalier, —an accomplished fact. The subsequent prayers in the desecrated church of St. Laure were, so far as the law was concerned, no more than the supererogatory works of good Catholics. But thither, to make assurance doubly sure, went the infatuated pair before the learned priest of Faye. He had neither surplice nor white stole, but he recited the appointed prayers in Latin; and though there was no holy water to sprinkle the intended husband and wife, and to cross the ring, the ring was there, and the gold and silver coins. The curé blessed the ring and the coins, and passed them on his book to Michel, who presented the money to Jacqueline (who let it drop out of her loose grasp), and, taking her passive hand, put the ring on her thumb, her forefinger, and her middle finger, in the name of the blessed Trinity,

leaving it on the third finger with the final Amen,
—a seal which no power less than that of the
Pope of Rome could break.

The book-worm priest cared nothing for the
transaction, so that his manuscripts and his brown
tomes were safe; and he pronounced the benediction with half an eye on his beloved haversack,
which, for the sake of space, he had in the form
of a pedlar's pack, now leaning against a pillar.

Michel had ordered the charrette to be yoked
and waiting near. He led his wife to it through
the boys of the pavement, and the women who
sat at work on the doorsteps. Without delay he
lifted her to her former seat, mounted himself,
and whipped the horse homeward. It was noon,
and the tell-tale breeze fluttered around and floated
away from the two whose lot in life was now so
strangely changed; and who still staggered blindly
and stupidly after the step they had taken, for
which there remained no remedy. Civil marriages
could indeed be broken as easily as contracted,
by mutual consent; but where then would be
honour, integrity, virginal purity of name and

fame? And the Church's sacraments could only be unloosed by the Church.

It was yet far from sunset when Michel Sart drew up with his bride in the entrance to his mother's auberge of Faye. The villagers were mostly at work getting in the last hay crop. There had been disturbance enough all the morning at the Tour, but it had not extended, beyond a few guarded inquiries, to the hamlet. Therefore if any one saw a cloaked figure in the charrette with Michel Sart, he was at liberty to suppose it was a chance countrywoman to whom he, with his usual benevolence, was giving a cast in his cart.

La Sarte, however, came out into the wide entrance at the rattle of the wheels. "Where have you been, my gaillard, without telling me?" cried the old woman, with vivacity; "so that I had your dinner prepared in vain. Heaven! it is the Demoiselle you have brought back. Mademoiselle, how they will rejoice themselves at the Tour! Babette was here for a second, asking if I had seen you. 'No,' I said. 'No; but she must have strayed, and lost her way.' Are you very tired, my poor Mademoiselle?"

"My old woman," interrupted Michel, laying his hand with unconscious heaviness on his mother's shoulder, "I never heard you a chatterer before, —but you help me. Say you that I have brought back Mademoiselle de Faye? No, my mother, I have brought back my wife from the mairie and the church of St. Laure at La Maille."

"Michel, what have you done? Oh! you hurt me!" cried his mother, writhing from underneath his heavy hand. Her fine cut face, which had been unusually bright at seeing him again after an unaccountable absence, that could yet bear no unwelcome interpretation, because it was her brave, big Michel who was concerned, grew haggard as from a deadly blow, taking all in at a word, a glance. There was brought home to her the forfeited trust, the utterly unequal, imprudent marriage, and, not least, the grievous slight, in the secrecy of the act, to her, his mother.

"Forgive me, my mother," entreated Michel, with a sorrowful humility and contrition in the midst of his success. "Consider, the deed is done and cannot be undone; and, because you are a good woman and my true mother, spare her."

La Sarte made a great effort: "It is done, my son; I say no more. I leave you to God and to the saints. May they have mercy on your frailty. I welcome my daughter. She is my daughter,— that is all now."

END OF VOL. I.

PRINTED BY J. AND W. RIDER, LONDON.

9 781331 759652